Cloneward
BOUND

J-FICTION

ALSO BY M.E. CASTLE

Popular Clone

OTHER EGMONT USA BOOKS
YOU MAY ENJOY

Guinea Dog
by Patrick Jennings

My Homework Ate My Homework
by Patrick Jennings

How to Grow Up and Rule the World
by Vordak the Incomprehensible

Cloneward BOUND

THE CLONE CHRONICLES #2

M.E. CASTLE

EGMONT
USA
New York

EGMONT

We bring stories to life

First published by Egmont USA, 2013
This paperback edition published by Egmont USA, 2013
443 Park Avenue South, Suite 806
New York, NY 10016

Copyright © Paper Lantern Lit, 2013

 paper lantern lit

1 3 5 7 9 8 6 4 2

www.egmontusa.com · www.theclonechronicles.com

THE LIBRARY OF CONGRESS HAS CATALOGED THE
HARDCOVER EDITION AS FOLLOWS

Castle, M. E.
Cloneward bound / M.E. Castle.
p. cm.—(The Clone chronicles ; #2)
Summary: After his clone escapes to Hollywood and becomes an actor, Fisher
Bas goes on a school trip to get him back before their secret is discovered.
ISBN 978-1-60684-233-1 (hardback)—ISBN 978-1-60684-405-2 (electronic book)
[1. Cloning--Fiction. 2. School field trips—Fiction. 3. Bullies—Fiction.
4. Middle schools--Fiction. 5. Schools—Fiction.] I. Title.
PZ7.C2687337Clo 2013
[Fic]—dc23
2012024613

Paperback ISBN 978-1-60684-473-1

Printed in the United States of America

For my sister,
As she steps out into the world.
I think I owe a warning . . . to the world.

Cloneward
BOUND

CHAPTER 1

It's a tough life, being a middle schooler.
You have to watch out for yourself.
Or, in my case, all of your selves.

— Fisher Bas, Journal

"Morning, Fisher!"

Fisher Bas smiled and waved at Jacob Li, then winced. His elbow ached. He was still getting used to saying hello to other kids. Up until about two weeks ago, his existence at Wompalog Middle School had barely been acknowledged— much less appreciated. Before then, his Monday morning was usually spent mathematically analyzing the layout of the decorative plants in the school's hallway, calculating the chances of being spotted as he dashed from one to another.

A lot can change in a few days. Fisher, once a stale bread crumb caught in the thin, scraggly stubble of middle school, had suddenly become a fresh, flaky croissant in the eyes of his classmates.

Fisher made his way down the hall, passing spots that would always stand as monuments to his past embarrassments: the Museum of Fisher's Pathetic Existence. First he passed infamous locker number 314, where he'd spent four entire class periods because he hadn't known that the inside latch was broken when he'd hidden in it.

Next, he passed the chipped double doors to the school library. He knew that if he inspected the larger books inside, a good half of them would have the faint imprint of his head. He winced whenever he walked past the encyclopedia shelf, and not just because the entry on particle physics was in dire need of an update. He'd offered to write it himself and glue his new entry over the current one, but the librarians hadn't been too pleased with the idea, which had baffled Fisher.

Leaving the library behind, he saw a line of metal coat hooks sticking out of the wall, one of which was bent crookedly toward the ground. Small as he was, Fisher weighed a lot more than a coat. The Vikings, the gang of bullies that had made his life a living nightmare since they had grown into hulking monstrosities in fourth grade, had held him down, stripped his coat off, and forced it on him backward. Then they'd pulled his hood up in front of his face and slipped it onto the hook.

"Well, well, well. What have we here?"

Fisher stopped dead in his tracks. He turned around, sneakers squeaking loudly, as if asking his permission to run away without him.

As though summoned by his thoughts, there they were: the looming, ugly faces of Brody, Willard, and Leroy. The

Vikings. They looked like statues cut from dark, grimy stone by a sculptor with no depth perception and very shaky hands.

Brody stood in the center as always, the leader of the pack. Willard bobbled back and forth slightly on clumsy, uneven legs on Brody's right, and to Brody's left stood Leroy. By far the dumbest and most easily distracted of the bunch, Leroy's eyes started to drift after a few seconds.

"Good morning, Fisher," Brody said with the least reassuring smile Fisher had ever seen. Alligators smiled with less malice. Fisher would know. His father kept one in the lab at home.

"Um . . . hello," Fisher said, trying to muster up some of his newfound courage. Unfortunately, when facing the Vikings, it was definitely not in the mood to be mustered.

Before the TechX episode, most people at Wompalog had settled for ignoring Fisher. But the Vikings had gone out of their way to notice—and torment—him. They were obviously displeased that Fisher's escaping from the famous TechX Industries—and exposing its dark secrets—had made him an overnight hero.

Now *everyone* noticed Fisher, and he was no longer such an easy target. But just because they had eased up a little lately did not mean that the threat was over.

"We're just giving you a friendly reminder," Brody said, rubbing his greasy palms together, "that we're still here."

"And things may *hic* be qu-quiet now," Willard went on, "but k-keep your ears open."

"We've, uh, got you under lobstervation," Leroy finished. Brody turned and gave him a long, withering look, then let out a frustrated sigh.

"Observation, Leroy," Brody said. He turned back to Fisher. "Now get out of here before we decide to make this chat a little more private. Maybe in that janitor's closet over there . . . ?"

Fisher looked to the closet in question and shivered. Unspeakable things had happened in the janitor's mop bucket, and he wanted no part of them. He didn't need a second invitation to flee.

"Lobstervation??" he heard Brody say as he sped away. "What do you think I want to do, turn him into a shellfish? Willard, if you please." The last thing Fisher heard before he turned the corner was the resounding *smack* of Willard's broad, fat hand against Leroy's broad, fat head.

He walked around the corner so fast that he ran smack into a kid he hadn't seen, half somersaulting forward and landing in a daze on his back.

"Oop. Sorry, Fisher," the boy said, helping Fisher to his feet. Fisher looked at the unfamiliar boy's acne-pitted, smiling face. The boy was obviously an eighth grader.

"No worries . . ." Fisher said, backing away. He still wasn't used to the idea that other people knew *him*.

Two weeks ago, an encounter with the Vikings would have ended with Fisher head down in a wastepaper basket or sifting the baseball field's dirt out of his hair. But ever since his trained attack mosquitoes had swarmed the Vikings in the middle of the cafeteria, they'd been a lot more careful around him. He'd earned a degree of respect around Wompalog that even the Vikings were forced to acknowledge.

Except *he* hadn't earned it. At least, he hadn't earned it alone. A feeling of guilt squirmed in the bottom of Fisher's stomach. As he headed to class, he reached into his pocket and withdrew a crumpled piece of paper. He unfolded it for the four hundred and fifty-fourth time— he'd counted—and read the note.

I went to find our mother and ended up in the gleaming land of Hollywood. I love it here! I bet you're wondering how I escaped the TechX blast. Can't wait to tell you the whole story. See you soon, brother.
—Two

5

Two, aka Fisher-2, a genetically exact copy of Fisher. A clone that Fisher had made himself, using an extremely secret, highly dangerous chemical compound, Accelerated Growth Hormone, that he'd stolen from his mom's personal lab. The last time he'd seen Two was in the collapsing corridors of TechX Industries, fighting with Dr. X: shadowy inventor, evil megalomaniac and, as it turned out, Fisher's (former) favorite biology teacher.

Moments later, the whole complex had turned into a hundred-foot-tall column of glowing dust. Naturally, Fisher had assumed that Two had gone down with the building and, as horrible as Fisher had felt about losing Two, he also felt a guilty sense of relief. If Two was gone, it meant that his secret was safe forever.

Now, it turned out that not only was his secret *not* safe, it was running around Los Angeles, chasing after a commercial actress who formed the center of the fantasy Fisher had hastily created to try and keep Two in check. Considering how much havoc Two had caused while loose in the school, Fisher could hardly imagine what kind of damage he could inflict in one of the biggest cities on earth.

Two school weeks had passed since TechX had gone up in an ash cloud, and Fisher had ridden the waves of glory well enough until Friday, when the note appeared in his mailbox. He'd spent all weekend in his room laboratory trying to construct a Two Tracking Unit. After a mind-numbing process of figuring out how to make it not just point at himself, he took the TTU out for a test run. Unfortunately, all it had pointed him in the direction of was an opossum, a 1992 Honda Civic, and a hot dog with peppers. Maybe if he could figure out what trace elements Two had in common with those things . . .

Fisher refolded the note for the four hundred and fifty-fourth time and tucked it back into his pocket. He tried to will away mental images of the HOLLYWOOD sign blasting into space, Two perched happily in one of the crooks of the W. Fisher turned into his science classroom and took his usual seat at the front left corner.

Every day for a year, he had walked into this room and sat down in exactly the same spot, while skinny, meek Mr. Granger had tried (mostly unsuccessfully) to get the class in order. Fisher had gotten to know Granger and even considered him a friend. Fisher was a genius. He had also learned, over the past few weeks, that he was a pretty good liar. This meant, he thought, that he should be a pretty good lie *detector*.

But it turned out that his biology teacher had really been a fiendish, maniacal scientist bent on destruction and conquest, and Fisher hadn't even had a clue. It made him wonder if any of his other teachers were really super-villains. He could definitely see his English teacher, Mrs.

Weedle, fitting the bill. If Mr. Granger had been able to hide his true nature from Fisher for so long, what kind of secrets could the other people around him be hiding? He let his eyes wander around the classroom.

But as he glanced toward the door, his mind went blank, and his lungs decided to take a quick mid-inhale break.

Veronica Greenwich walked through the door trailing a blur of dawn light and silver mist—at least, that's what it seemed like to Fisher. She saw him and smiled, and Fisher was just able to muster enough control over his face muscles to smile back.

Fisher hadn't told anyone that Granger was actually Dr. X and had been disintegrated along with the TechX building. Who would have believed him, anyway? As far as Fisher was concerned, all that mattered was that after Mr. Granger had "mysteriously disappeared," there had been some reshuffling of the science classes, and he was now in the same class as Veronica.

After she sat down on the other side of the room, Fisher slipped another piece of paper out of his bag and set it on his desk, then pulled out a pencil.

Increase in social acknowledgement following TechX incident over time passed since, respect among scientific peers, reputation among students helped with homework . . . He scribbled in a few new variables and numbers.

Taking into account recent actions of V—Veronica, in the equations—a careful measure of smiling ratio should yield answer . . . K.

On the far right side of the equation, the point of all Fisher's tangled math and logic, was the letter K.

K: the exact moment in time when Fisher might get his first kiss from Veronica.

K: the idea was something so otherworldly to Fisher that the only way he could cope with it was in a form that he understood: symbols, variables, and strings of numbers. It was the way that he best understood the world. At the same time, he knew that, if it happened, the kiss itself wasn't going to take place on graph paper. And if—when!—an opportunity for K should arise, he didn't know *what* he would do. Was there a book he could read? Somebody he could ask?

His pencil worked like it had a mind of its own—and a frantic mind at that. The layers of equations scrawled along and filled out as Fisher added new variables to account for Veronica's recent behavior toward him. At first, when he'd embraced his new hero status, she had coldly shrugged him off. But he could tell that the new result was going to yield a much smaller value for K. He felt his face begin to go slack as the last few results added up.

He stared down at the new value of K. He blinked once.

K = Time until I kiss Veronica

$$\frac{i + (p+s)}{t} + \frac{V_s + V_d}{t - t_l} = K$$

let:

i = Increase in social acknowledgement
   following TechX incident

t = time in hours

p = respect among scientific peers

s = reputation among students helped
   with homework

V_s = number of smiles exchanged with Veronica

V_d = average smile duration in milliseconds
   (see log)

t_l = time spent in locker, in hours

~~1698.27~~

$$\frac{i + (p+s)}{t} + \frac{V_s + V_d}{t - t_l} = \boxed{1214.008}$$

The number had indeed decreased by almost fifty percent—to only one thousand, two hundred fourteen years, and three days. He looked back over at Veronica as she neatly wrote the date at the top of her class notes. *Maybe if I put both of us into long-term hibernation incryo-freeze pods . . .*

"Good morning, everyone!"

Fisher was taken out of his reverie by the voice of Ms. Snapper, Mr. Granger's replacement. She normally taught eighth-grade science, but had agreed to take over Mr. Granger's class until further notice. Fisher quickly folded up his graph paper and slipped it into his bag.

Ms. Snapper was tall and slender, wore black, wire-frame glasses, and had dark brown hair pulled back into a ponytail. Since she had stepped in to teach the class after Mr. Granger's mysterious disappearance, Fisher had gotten to like her. Still, he had liked Mr. Granger, too, and look how *that* had ended up. He was going to need some more time before he could feel at ease in this class, no matter who taught it.

"I've got a special announcement to make," Ms. Snapper said in a bright, cheerful voice. "You may remember Mr. Granger was planning a trip this week," she said. "In spite of the . . . unfortunate circumstances," she went on—none of the teachers seemed sure how to talk about Mr. Granger's vanishing act—"I spoke to the administration and we're going to go ahead with our class trip to LA, where we'll get the privilege of seeing a taping of the popular TV program *Strange Science*! We'll depart midday this Friday and be back on Monday morning in time for third period."

Several people shouted and clapped; others sighed, clearly annoyed at the prospect of giving up a weekend for anything school related. Fisher felt like he could bounce out of his seat. He'd forgotten all about the proposed trip in light of the whole clone situation. Two was in LA! Now Fisher had a way to get there. This could be his chance to find his clone . . . before everyone else found out about him.

As an added bonus, *Strange Science* had become a late-afternoon favorite of his since it started airing. That was largely due to its host, who went by the name Dr. Devilish. He was tall and handsome, with a commanding presence and a smooth-talking charm—*and* he was an accomplished scientist. Fisher had never seen someone who had both academic and social skills. Dr. Devilish gave him hope for his own future.

"Because this trip takes place over the weekend," Ms. Snapper went on, "participation is strictly voluntary. So, can I get a show of interested students?"

Fisher's hand shot up first, and others followed. Some people were murmuring excitedly about Dr. Devilish;

others were obviously looking forward to missing half of Friday and two class periods on Monday.

Then Fisher saw Veronica's hand go up. His pulse started thudding. It was too good to be true. He quickly reached down and whipped out his graph paper. He scribbled with one hand as he kept the other up, trying to determine how going on this trip together might affect the value of K. Hopefully, enough to make it earlier than the year that Wompalog Middle School became an archaeological dig site.

"Ms. Snapper?" said Veronica.

"Yes . . . Veronica?" Ms. Snapper said, taking a moment to be sure she had her name right. "You have a question?"

"Is . . ." Veronica looked slightly embarrassed. "Do you think there's any chance we might get to meet Kevin Keels?"

Fisher dropped his pencil.

"Kevin Keels . . ." Ms. Snapper said, her eyes turning up in thought. "Is that an actor you like?"

Fisher felt like he'd just been slapped in the face with a frozen mackerel. Kevin Keels was the latest pop sensation, a thirteen-year-old whose ballads and dance hits were slowly creeping on to every radio station nationwide, as Veronica—as well as all the other girls in the class— hurried to explain to Ms. Snapper. The only reason Fisher

13

knew about the pop star's existence was that CURTIS, the artificial intelligence he'd freed from TechX that now resided in his computer, had been wailing Keels's incredibly annoying and brain-meltingly stupid songs for the past three weeks straight. And to top it off, Kevin Keels had just finished filming a movie about his rise to fame: *Keel Me Now*.

Which was more or less the thought that went through Fisher's head as he buried it in his hands, trying to drown out the excited chatter that filled the room.

≋ CHAPTER 2 ≋

If the monkey really wanted to get the weasel, he would've stopped wasting time and burned down the mulberry bush.

—Amanda Cantrell,
Practice Harvard Admissions Essay

By the time science class ended, Fisher felt as though his heart was plastered to the soles of his shoes. Kevin Keels? Kevin Keels, whose hair actually glowed as if a helicopter with a spotlight followed him everywhere he went. Kevin Keels, who sold out arenas so big you needed an astronomical telescope to see him from the back row. Kevin Keels, who had a basketball shoe named after him *even though he didn't play basketball.*

Kevin Keels! Really?! Fisher fumed. His music was cheesier than a map of Wisconsin cut from a four-cheese pizza. And how could an accomplished English student like Veronica get so—*blushy*—over someone who had a hit single titled "Not Never Wouldn't Leave You"?

He had just stepped into the hall and had started toward his next class when he was seized by a hand on his left shoulder.

As Fisher found himself spun roughly around, he

fumbled into his back pocket, preparing to defend himself with his Instant Nose Froster.

Then he saw Amanda Cantrell's angry face and stopped mid-draw. The tiny plastic device was knocked from his hand. As it collided with a bank of lockers, the Nose Froster let out a fine plume of white spray, turning a passing sixth grader's nasal passages into a miniature model of a glacier formation.

The girl let out something between a scream and a honk, her arms flailing as she ran toward the nearest bathroom.

"Amanda!" he cried out in surprise, choking a bit as she pinned him against the locker. "Is, uh . . . something wrong?"

"Something is *very* wrong," she said, her dark hair whipping around her face like deadly vines. She freed one hand to adjust the black-rimmed glasses that her ambush had jostled out of place. The other arm was more than enough to keep Fisher pinned. Amanda was short, but she was *strong*. She was head of the debate team *and* captain of the wrestling team. "And you're going to tell me what."

"What—what are you talking about?" stuttered Fisher. Little beads of sweat rolled down the back of his neck.

"When you started acting weird a few weeks ago, I was confused, but I figured you had finally evolved from a sea slug into some kind of vertebrate." Apparently, Fisher's

Instant Nose Froster

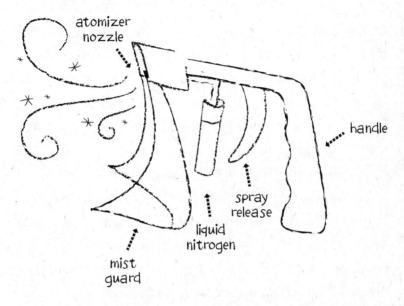

atomizer nozzle

handle

spray release

liquid nitrogen

mist guard

new fame hadn't made people forget about his father's Bas-Hermaphrodite-Sea-Slug Hypothesis. Fisher tried to wriggle away from her grasp, but there was no escape. He was at Amanda's mercy. *"Then* you crawled out of TechX completely unhurt, even though the whole place blew sky-high moments earlier—"

"Look, Amanda, if we could maybe—"

"After you came back to school, you were right-handed, even though you'd been left-handed the week before. And you have a third freckle on your nose that I *know* wasn't there before."

Fisher's eyes darted around the hallway, willing someone to help him. But the few people left in the hall were busy at their own lockers or shot a terrified glance at Amanda before scurrying away. He'd never had help when the Vikings bullied him. He wasn't going to get it now that Amanda practically had him in a headlock.

"You understand how these events conflict, don't you? Did you think no one would notice?" Her steely eyes bore into Fisher. He could practically feel a little burning spot on his forehead. His knees were beginning to twitch.

"L-listen," he said, struggling frantically for excuses, "I know a lot of weird things have happened, but I don't know what you're—*ow*!" Her fingers dug into his left shoulder as she fished a smart phone out of her pocket. She held the screen inches from his face.

"Shut up and watch," she said, and with a few rapid flicks of her fingers, pulled up a video on her phone.

The screen faded up on a simple setup: a small room with blank walls and floor, and a chair in the middle.

A chair in which Fisher was sitting.

Only it wasn't Fisher. It was Two. Showing his face—*Fisher's* face!—on camera.

"We here at Spot-Rite have been getting your spots right out for over ten years now," Two was saying chirpily. It was an audition tape for a commercial. "And as long as there are spots to get out, we will continue to provide the best cleaning product available." Two went on to talk about the newest Spot-Rite product—a cleaner that was nontoxic and edible, so parents wouldn't have to worry about cleaning a counter with it and contaminating their food. He then had a three-person discussion about the product, with two sock puppets dressed as kittens. The puppets began to dance in the air to prerecorded music as Two sang a jingle.

But the real kicker was when a third puppet—this one, a dog—came into the shot. Was Two operating a sock puppet with each hand and a *foot*? The clone's talents and abilities were matched only by the insanity of the things he chose to use them for.

Fisher's eyes skated frantically to the stats posted below the video. For a moment, he thought he was going to pass out. The video had already gotten ten thousand views in three days. The first comment was: awwww SO CUTE. the cats aren't bad either loling.

"See the time stamp in the bottom left corner?" Amanda said. Fisher just managed to nod. "This video was filmed three days ago, at eight fifty in the morning. When you were sitting in Ms. Snapper's class *right in front of me.*"

"You don't understand—I mean, I don't understand— I mean, there's an explanation—" He wished he could argue logically, but he knew he sounded like he was having a panic attack with a duck call in his mouth.

"Save it, Fisher." She shook him once, hard. "I want the truth and nothing but the truth."

"Okay, okay." He held up both hands in surrender. He knew that Amanda and Two had become close when the clone had been in school. Ever since Fisher had crawled from the ruins of TechX, Amanda had been watching him like a hawk, observing the way he acted and spoke. She looked like she was keeping a catalogue of every move he made in her hard drive of a brain. He couldn't keep the truth from her, but maybe he could keep her from spreading it. "I'll tell you the truth, but can we go somewhere else?"

Amanda let Fisher go and pointed to the same supply closet Brody had threatened him with. Forcing images of the janitor's mop bucket from his mind, Fisher nodded reluctantly.

"In," she said. Fisher checked to make sure the hall was clear, and they slipped into the closet.

"Okay," Amanda said, even more intimidating in the dim, harsh light of the closet's tiny, uncovered light-bulb. "Who was sitting in class the day that video was filmed?"

"Fisher," Fisher said, a tiny squeak popping up into his throat. He swallowed. "Me."

"And who made that video?"

"Fisher . . . Two." Fisher clenched his eyes closed and

gritted his teeth. Finally. He had said it. The secret was out.

"Fisher, I just said you couldn't have done both," Amanda replied, leaning closer threateningly.

"No, no," he said, "not *too* like also. *Two*. The number two."

Amanda stared at him for a moment.

"There's more than one of you," she said, completely deadpan.

"Two, to be exact," Fisher said, "and that's what I call him. Two. I . . . made him. In my bedroom." Amanda raised an eyebrow so high, it threatened to zip off her forehead and embed itself in the ceiling. Fisher sighed and, stuttering, told her the whole story of Two's life: his mother's Accelerated Growth Hormone, growing Two in a tank in his room, and the events leading up to the destruction of TechX Enterprises. He also told her about how Two had seen a Spot-Rite commercial on television the moment he "woke up" and become obsessed with the idea that the actress in it was his mother. The only thing he carefully left out was the fact that Dr. X had used an android looking exactly like Amanda to lure Two in.

He'd lied to Two to keep him under control. He'd told him that they were on a covert mission to rescue their mother and that the middle school was a training ground for the evil organization that they were fighting against. Fisher didn't know how much of it Two really still believed after what they went through at TechX (he was, after all, as brilliant as Fisher), but if he was auditioning to be the new face of Spot-Rite, there was a pretty good chance he still believed the Spot-Rite actress was his mother.

When he'd finally let everything out, he actually felt kind of relieved, like he'd been carrying a sack of rocks everywhere he went and he'd just thrown a few of them away.

"Listen to me," Fisher said. "This can't get out. I was almost killed trying to keep Two's existence a secret. I didn't even know he escaped TechX until a few days ago, but he could be in serious danger if anyone else finds him. I need you to promise you'll tell no one. If Two's in LA, I have a chance to get to him before he blows this secret wide open."

Amanda leaned in very close and looked Fisher straight in the eyes. Fisher would have backed away, but he was already pressed up against the shelves of toilet paper and the weird powder janitors use when kids puke in the hall-way. For a second, he thought Amanda might head-butt him. He gulped.

"Hmm." Amanda backed away and held out her hand. She seemed to have made her decision. Fisher breathed a sigh of relief and shook it, trying not to wince at the strength of her grip.

"If it was anyone else but you, I wouldn't believe it. But I think you're telling the truth," Amanda said. "If your secret is putting Two . . . and you," she added grudgingly, "in danger, I'll help you get him back. On one condition."

". . . Okay," Fisher said, feeling a pulse of anxiety. He was glad to have the help, but he couldn't imagine what Amanda's condition would be. His thoughts flew wildly through possibilities. Would she blackmail him into paying her a secret-keeping fee for the rest of his life? Would she make him do all of her science homework forever? Would she want him to create an Amanda Two?

"Convince him to be my date for the fall formal."

Fisher was momentarily speechless.

"You want to take him to a *dance*?" he finally choked out. "That's your condition? Have you listened to a word I've said?"

"Don't get any ideas," she snapped quickly. "I don't *like* him or anything like that. But it's one of the biggest events of the year and he's the only boy around that I could put up with for an entire evening."

"But, but . . . I can't guarantee that I'll be able to convince him," Fisher said. "I can't tell him what to do.

Besides, I was going to ask Veronica to the formal. And I already explained that *both* Fishers can't go to the dance."

"I gave you my condition," Amanda said. "What you do about it is your problem." With that, she took him by the elbow, spun him around, and pushed him out of the closet.

≋ CHAPTER 3 ≋

Plan A rarely works. Save time, and start with Plan C.

—Vic Daring (Issue #218)

Fisher arrived home still trembling. He couldn't believe that his deepest, darkest secret was no longer his alone. He felt a slight tingle as he walked through the Liquid Door of the front gate, passing through it as if it were mist. Someone with DNA the house didn't recognize would bounce off it like they'd hit a brick wall.

As terrifying as the confrontation with Amanda had been, he still felt a sense of relief. It had felt good to tell the truth. And Amanda had volunteered to help. He had a chance to find Two again. He could set everything right.

He walked between clusters of volleyball-size grapes clinging to vines as wide as Fisher's entire body. The latest addition to his mother's experimental garden was faring well. A French vineyard had signed a contract with Mrs. Bas, since just two of her grapes would yield a full bottle of wine. Plus, they provided a place for his father's newest batch of landlobsters to live and play.

As Fisher pushed open the door, he stopped and sighed.

His father was in the foyer, hopping on one foot trying to untangle his suspenders from his left ankle. His mother's head was bent sideways because one dangly earring had gotten caught in her necklace chain.

His parents could alter genetic structures with their eyes closed. They could design ovens that could discuss geopolitics while broiling chicken. But they could barely dress themselves in normal clothing, much less *act* like normal human beings.

"Hey, there, Fisher," his dad said, between hops.

"Welcome home, sweetie," his mom said. The way her head was twisted made her look like a confused bird.

"Hey, Mom. Hey, Dad," Fisher said with a sigh. "Big night out?"

"We're going to the symphony," his dad said, freeing himself from his own suspenders only to hook his cuff-links together. He walked toward Fisher with his wrists bound together. "Could you give me a hand, Fisher?"

"Sure," Fisher said, reaching up and trying to figure out how his father had managed to handcuff himself with only a pair of fancy buttons. He looked up at his dad's disheveled mop. "Your hair looks a little, um . . ." He gestured with his hands, since what he really wanted to say was, *Your hair looks like an iguana's nest after a hurricane.*

"Yes," his dad replied, trying to help free his hands. "I

was trying to apply my hair gel but FP jumped up and ate it."

"What?!" Fisher said. "Is he okay?"

"Don't worry, it's perfectly safe to eat—though I can't imagine it tastes very good. He'll be fine."

"Well, okay," Fisher said, "I guess if . . ." His eyes drifted up past his father's head. "Um, are you *sure* he'll be okay?"

"It's completely nontoxic," his dad said, finally freeing his wrists. "Why?"

"Because he appears to be glued to the ceiling." Fisher pointed.

The family pet, and Fisher's best friend, was named Flying Pig, usually called FP. Fisher's mother had engineered the little fellow, a small pig with flaps under his forelegs that served as wings. He couldn't really fly, but he was a pretty talented glider.

One thing he was not, however, was self-adhesive. Yet there he was, stuck to the ceiling like a twitchy pink mushroom.

"FP!" Mrs. Bas exclaimed, looking around for something to get him down with.

"You okay, boy?" Fisher called up to him. FP made a few squeaks. He sounded more annoyed than pained.

"Oh dear," Mr. Bas said, scratching his head. "I should have guessed. The gel is made of adaptive materials. Its

SELF-INSERTING/CLIPPING CUFFLINKS

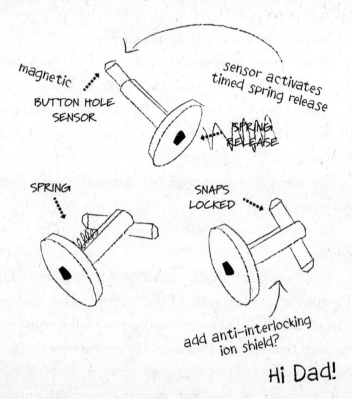

magnetic

BUTTON HOLE SENSOR

sensor activates timed spring release

SPRING RELEASE

SPRING

SNAPS LOCKED

add anti-interlocking ion shield?

Hi Dad!

strength adjusts to its environment. FP's body must be cranking the gel all the way up and sweating it out."

Fisher found a long-handled broom and with a great effort managed to pry FP from the ceiling. FP squealed as he flailed his legs, trying to slow his descent to the floor. He hit with a thud—and his backside immediately attached itself to the linoleum. But at least he was on the floor.

Mr. Bas shook his head. "Well, this is a pickle. If the gel is in his system, he could be sweating it out for days. He'll stick to anything he touches."

Fisher sighed and poked at FP until his hooves were on the floor. His whole body was glistening with the powerful gel.

"I guess I'll try and work up an antidote," Fisher said, dropping his backpack on the floor and pulling out a folder. "Before you go, could one of you sign this permission slip? My science class is taking a field trip this weekend to LA."

His mother, still halfway out of one shoe, hopped over and took the slip from Fisher.

"Oh!" she said, reading it over. "You're going to a taping of *Strange Science*?" She bit her lower lip absently. Then she said with false casualness, "I think I'll volunteer for one of the chaperone spots. Because, that is . . ." She thought for a moment. "Well, LA is a big place, after all, and it can be dangerous. I should insist on accompanying you."

"Hmph," Fisher's dad replied. "You just want to get a chance to meet that Dr. Devilish. He's nothing but a phony with a silly goatee and a too-tight lab coat. I bet he couldn't reverse engineer an electron spectrometer if he had the instructions tattooed on his big, manly hands. He's not a real scientist. Or even a real actor! He just smiles at the camera, and everybody loves it. If you're going to see a show produced, you should see *Sci-Fi: Survivor!*"

"Sci-fi *what*?" Fisher's mom asked. She was blushing, and Fisher noticed she had not tried to deny that she wanted to see Dr. Devilish.

"A new show. It's premiering next week. A group of people are put in a maze full of challenges based on different sci-fi genres, and they have to figure out clever ways to get past them. Now that's a show where people really have to use their heads! Critical thinking, problem solving under pressure . . ."

"Oh, *that* show," his mom said disdainfully. "It's only getting hype because it comes on right before *Strange Science*," his mom fired back. "So Fisher, about that—"

"Er, sorry," Fisher said quickly. "All the chaperone spots are taken."

"Oh," Mrs. Bas said, clearly crestfallen. "Well, I'm sure it'll be a rewarding experience."

There was a brief moment of awkward silence. Fisher's mom finally managed to free her earring.

"So," Fisher said, attempting to change the subject, "what's the occasion, anyway? You almost never have nights out."

His parents looked at each other, and his mother let out a long sigh.

"I wasn't going to tell you right away, because I didn't want you to worry about me," she said. "But . . . due to setbacks and security risks, my AGH project has been shut down. I was ordered to hand over all samples of the chemical I'd kept in the lab." For a moment, Fisher's mom looked as though she might cry. "I kept a precise log of all of my supplies . . . but I still came up a centiliter short."

"It's not your fault," Mr. Bas said, putting a hand on his wife's arm.

Fisher folded his hands behind his back, then proceeded to squeeze them until he thought his fingers would break. One one-hundredth of a liter of AGH. Exactly the amount that he had used to create Two. Not only did his mother know that it was missing—so did the government.

"How . . . how do you think that might have happened?" he asked, struggling to keep his voice steady.

"I don't know," she admitted. "It could have been as simple as a temperature change that caused a little bit to evaporate. Or maybe I incorrectly recorded the amounts. The fact of the matter is that the AGH is extremely powerful—and practically untested. For all we know, one centiliter could be used to engineer whole armies! The agency is extremely unhappy—I'm lucky I still have a job."

"You're the best scientist they've got," Mr. Bas said valiantly.

Mrs. Bas gave him a weak smile. "Be that as it may,

the bureau is terrified. After Dr. X's attempts to steal my formula, they believe it's possible that someone succeeded in removing a sample. They've dispatched whole teams to investigate a possible security breach. If someone stole the AGH, he'll be found, and caught . . . and hopefully thrown into a jail cell to rot," she finished fiercely.

"Uh . . . huh," stammered Fisher. He could almost feel the cold concrete cell pressing around him.

"Anyway, I just need a night to relax," she chirped, suddenly cheerful again, "and get away from it for a little bit. I've been answering some *very* personal questions about our family and my methods all week. They've finally cleared me of culpability, but it was a very stressful experience." Then she bent down, placing her hands on Fisher's shoulders. "Listen, Fisher. I don't know how long this investigation is going to last or whether any agents are going to come to the house to investigate further, but I don't want you to worry about it, okay? I'll be fine."

"That's good," Fisher said as his vision blurred and the room started spinning. He thought he might faint. Through the haze, he saw his parents headed for the door. "Have a good time," he said under his breath. It took his parents several tries to make it out the door, because Mr. Bas's silk scarf and Mrs. Bas's shawl managed to wreathe together and tie them up neck to neck.

When the door closed, Fisher stayed in place, not even

32

wavering, like he'd been nailed to the floorboards.

He had no idea how long he had been standing there when a crash from the kitchen made him whip around. He slipped up to the doorway and eased his head around, expecting to see a tall man in a black suit and sunglasses punching down the wall in pursuit of Fisher for his crimes.

Thankfully, the noise turned out to be a package of soup crackers that had been set down too close to the counter's edge.

"Young Fisher," came a voice straight out of a Charles Dickens novel. It sounded like an English butler, but was, in fact, the toaster.

"Oh, hi, Lord Burnside," Fisher said, relieved. "Have a good day?"

"Well, I must confess that this morning I slightly over-crisped a slice of whole wheat. I'm afraid that dreadful blunder put me in the darkest of moods for much of the day. Luckily, your father likes his toast dark so at least my foul mood produced something of worth. But if I cannot reliably and consistently perform my function, what good am I?" Lord Burnside had small glowing spots on his side that served to indicate eyes, and they dipped into a melancholy frown.

"I wouldn't let it get you down," Fisher said, inching once again toward the hallway. He needed to think. He needed a plan. "After all, just think how many pieces of bread would be left completely untoasted if it wasn't for your hard work!"

"Dear me," the little appliance said, eyespots growing wider. "All of that poor, cold, utterly uncrunchy bread! That would be disastrous. Indeed, perhaps I exaggerated the importance of one mistake, compared to the vast amount of important work that I do. Thank you, young sir. You have provided a very valuable perspective on the matter."

"Anytime, your lordship," Fisher said. He took the stairs to his room two at a time, slammed the door, and sagged against it.

His eyes landed on the cover of *Issue #412* of Vic Daring, Space Scoundrel, lying open and facedown on his bed. The artwork depicted the rakish adventurer catapulting himself free of a wrecked ship in a sleek chrome space suit, hurtling into black space, with no idea where the desperate escape might take him.

Fisher empathized. He, too, had to hurtle himself into the terrifying black space . . . of Los Angeles.

Twenty minutes later, Fisher was standing in front of a suitcase, which was, at the moment, still empty except for a solar-powered umbrella, a device that Fisher hadn't really thought through before he made it. Fortunately, it worked very well as a portable power source whenever it wasn't actually raining.

"Oh boy! LA! City of Angels! The bright lights! The stars! The big time! Prowlin' the mean streets!"

Once again, Fisher was conversing with a machine. It was CURTIS, Fisher's AI companion. CURTIS sounded like a pizza delivery guy from Brooklyn, but he had an extremely powerful computing mind.

CURTIS had spent most of his time on the TechX mainframe being very bored, and so had downloaded vast amounts of TV from the Internet. It was all he'd really known of the outside world before Fisher had taken him. Now he was giving Fisher advice on all the sights to check out in LA.

FP was taking careful steps around the room, trying not to touch anything that wasn't already secured to the floor. He wasn't doing a great job. The gel hadn't worn off yet, and two cough-drop wrappers and a crumpled-up page of Fisher's calculations were stuck to his legs.

"I'm not going to sightsee, CURTIS," Fisher said, looking through his sock drawer until he found his special, super-elastic, jump-enhancing socks. "I have important work to do when I get there."

"You know something, kid? One time, Dr. Devilish made a levitating platform with electromagnets and then played a guitar solo on top of it!"

"I'm pretty sure the music was prerecorded," Fisher

35

said, feeling along the upper shelf in his closet. He pulled down the camouflaging spray that he'd used to hide from the guards in TechX, along with a bagful of instant shrub seeds, which would sprout into a full-sized shrub within seconds of being watered.

"The legendary Hollywood Boulevard! The stars in the pavement! Bogart! Brando! And then there's Grauman's Chinese Theatre! Do you know what that place was like when *Star Wars* first came out? It was amazing, the displays of—"

"CURTIS!" Fisher shouted, spinning around to face the computer. "I'm not going there to look at movie stars or gawk at buildings. I've got to find Two."

Fisher tucked a necktie into his suitcase. It was made of a material that would expand and stretch up to twenty times its length. That was a device Fisher had invented by accident; all he'd wanted when he made it was a necktie that he could successfully knot in a half Windsor without strangling himself.

The computer made a sighing sound.

"Fine, fine." He chuckled a few times before going silent.

"Sometimes I miss only having a toaster to talk to," Fisher mumbled to himself, zipping his suitcase closed.

Hours later, Fisher sat on the edge of his bed, a clipboard in one hand and a pencil in the other. He knew he should be trying to sleep, but he'd been turning and shifting so much that FP had leapt from the bed and perched, asleep, on Fisher's in-progress Tesla coil, hidden under a draped sheet next to his desk. Fisher hadn't mentioned to his parents that he'd been trying to construct an artificial lightning-bolt maker. His mother would overreact he was sure.

Fisher's pencil flew frantically across the paper until it was warm in his hand. He wrote out dozens of equations about the mission ahead. First, he took the population of Los Angeles, the city's size, and a few other factors, and calculated the odds that he would step off the bus and run right into Two. He hadn't seen that many zeros to the right of a decimal since he'd fallen asleep on his keyboard with his nose on the 0 key.

He also made a few entertaining calculations just to ease his mind. The density of King of Hollywood franchises in the city, which was higher than the density of *humans* in some Midwestern states. The odds that, at any given moment, a seagull would land on his head. He didn't actually know enough about the behavior of seagulls for that one, so he assumed that human heads looked really comfy to seagulls.

He had just set the clipboard down and picked up the Two Tracking Unit to work out its kinks when three knocks sounded at his door.

"Can I come in, Fisher?" said his mother's voice.

"Sure," Fisher said as he attempted to leap back into his bed and look calm, but ended up looking like an over-caffeinated spider.

The door opened, and she walked in as Fisher tried to untangle himself from his top sheet.

"How was the orchestra?" Fisher asked as his mom sat down on the bed.

"Very good," she said. "I've always been a Stravinsky fan. Listen, Fisher . . . the government shutdown of my project is serious." Fisher nodded as slowly and placidly as he could. "I don't know how some of the AGH went unaccounted for. It's possible that I made an error somewhere or that something in my equipment was off. And that's probably what happened. But I still have to consider all the possibilities." She turned to look Fisher directly in the eyes.

"Like . . . what?" Fisher asked, hearing FP shift in his sleep and wishing he would swoop down and fly Fisher out the window.

"Someone might have taken it," his mom answered. "Dr. X had plenty of people working for him. It's even possible that kidnapping you"—there was a slight hitch in her voice—"was just a diversion, to get your father and me out of the house so that his spies could slip in and steal it. But I just don't know."

It took a moment for Fisher to understand the mixture of suspicion and gentleness in her expression. She suspected him. But at the same time, she'd lived through the terror of having him kidnapped and not knowing if she'd ever see him again.

Fisher felt pins of guilt sticking him in the ribs, but not hard enough to make him talk. It would be one thing if he'd taken some AGH to study it or to try and make himself taller. But there was another Fisher running around, and he wasn't ready to see either of his parents' reaction to that.

So he cleared his throat and said, "Who knows? Dr. X was capable of a lot. I saw that when I was inside TechX. I'm just sorry you had your project canceled."

"It's all right," his mom said, sighing and standing up. "When I began to realize the possibilities for the project, I started to regret ever having done it. And the government knows just how dangerous the stuff is. The teams they dispatched to track the AGH down have been ordered to destroy anything it was used to create or alter. They're even confiscating and destroying the giant plants I made when I was testing a prehuman version of it."

Fisher felt his breath catch in his throat like a fishhook.

"Good night, Fisher," his mom said, walking to the door.

". . . G . . . night," Fisher managed to push out as she closed it behind her.

A lot of things had been on the line before. Now, everything was. If he failed, not only could he be arrested and imprisoned . . . Two could be killed.

CHAPTER 4

"School bus" is the normally used term because "asylum on wheels" is considered impolite.

—Fisher Bas, Personal Notes

A big, white spitball sailed over the seats like an artillery shell over a trench. The hum of conversation had swollen to a deafening roar, and small objects whizzed back and forth without warning. During the seven-hour trip to LA, the shouting, cascades of Cheetos and spilled Pepsis, and flying, spittle-encrusted pieces of notebook paper, had quickly turned the bus into a mobile trash heap.

In other words, it was just like any other Wompalog Friday, only in a small, cramped space from which there was no escape.

Fisher had hoped he'd be able to talk to Veronica during the trip. Not helping his cause was the fact that seats had been assigned, and she was sitting two rows in front of him, next to Trevor Weiss. Fisher could only imagine what they were talking about. Trevor's two favorite subjects were his collection of handmade pencil cases and the history of trout fishing.

Another spitball nearly grazed Fisher's head. He had

spent time working on a quickly deploying anti-spitball shield system, but he hadn't figured out a way to get the reaction time right, and tests had ended with the shield smacking him in the head as often as the spitballs.

As soon as his head had hit the pillow the night before, visions of dark-suited figures, eyeless behind pitch-black sunglasses, had filled his head. They chased him around street corners. They chased him through dark forests. He had even, at one point, tried to dive into a lake and swim to safety, only to be pursued by a sinister agent riding a giant grouper.

What if the investigation led to him and Two? Would Fisher be locked in a military laboratory and forced to make more clones? Would Two be cryogenically frozen while teams of researchers analyzed his chemical composition and cellular structure?

Then a still more chilling thought hit him. Fisher had made Two. What if he was forced to lead the team that took Two apart? He couldn't imagine accepting the task. But what would they do to him when he refused?

It was an unexpected relief when Ms. Snapper decided to play a documentary on earthworms to "entertain and enlighten." It was doing neither, but it was, at least, helping to keep Fisher out of his head.

"And so, with the coming of the April storm, the soil becomes saturated and the noble creatures, knowing their peaty homes shall soon flood, inch ever upward until they majestically break the surface and look blindly upon the cloudy sky. . . ." The whining monotone of the narrator's voice was barely audible, but still loud enough to be annoying.

Fisher poked his head cautiously above his seat, straining to see even a bit of Veronica's beautiful golden hair. But his field of vision was filled almost instantaneously by the head of Warren Deveraux, which popped up like a champagne cork.

"Hey, Fisher! Nice bus, huh? It's got screens and everything! Hey, d'ya think we can actually get TV on here, or just videos? And look how clean the windows are! I bet they wash them twice a day. What do you think? Twice? Maybe three times?"

Warren was a boy with exactly two settings: on and off. Fisher had learned this well.

"How about the cushions?" Fisher said. "Are they comfy enough?"

Warren popped back into his seat to investigate.

"Wow, yeah, this is—*zzzzzz* . . ."

Fisher shook his head.

"Fisher! Hey! We need to plan!" Amanda snapped her fingers in front of his face. Fisher turned to her sheepishly.

"Sorry," Fisher said. "I was, uh, seeing if the earthworm made it out of the ground."

"Uh-huh," Amanda said, jotting something down in a spiral notebook on her lap. She gave him a quick glare before turning back to her planning. "Look. LA is a big city. It's going to be hard enough to find Two even *with* a good plan."

"What have you come up with so far?" Fisher leaned against the window. His eyes drifted back to Veronica, or what little he could see of her (mostly an elbow).

Amanda chewed on the end of her pen thoughtfully. "What about the studio that's casting the new commercial?" she said, writing the word *STUDIO* in the center of her notes. "Two must have sent his video along to them. They might have a phone number for him or something."

"Good thinking," Fisher said. "I could get that personal info if I pretended to be his twin brother."

"You *are* his twin brother," Amanda said. "Just not the usual way."

Fisher took a moment to think about that. She was right; biologically, a clone was just an artificial twin. But more than that, before his disappearance, Fisher and Two had really started to become close. At first the difference in personality had made Fisher think that they could never coexist, but when they were fighting for their lives together, he'd realized how much they had in common. Now Two's life was in danger again and he didn't even know it.

DO NOT LOSE THIS, FISHER

Amanda's Battle Plan

MISSION: FIND TWO
LOCATION: LOS ANGELES, CA

Amanda Cantrell

He stretched his stiff neck, peering out the windows as he did, and his eyes paused on a sleek black car just behind and to the left of the bus. Its windows looked tinted . . . or was that just the reflection of the light?

Fisher sank lower into his seat. Were black-suited government agents watching him even now? Could they possibly know about Two?

But as he watched, the car began to drift farther away. Maybe Fisher was being paranoid. Would the agency really suspect a twelve-year-old of stealing the AGH from right under the nose of his genius mother?

All the same, Fisher slipped out of his seat and worked his way up the aisle, trying to see where the black car was going. Trevor shuffled past him toward the bathroom, his face a deep green. Fisher craned his neck to keep the car in sight. He had moved two rows forward when the bus swerved severely, with no warning at all. Fisher rocketed sideways . . . straight into Veronica's lap. The bus lurched a second time and came to a stop.

"Fisher!" Veronica said, surprise and concern equal in her voice. "Are you all right?"

Fisher froze, wide-eyed, his brain shouting five contradictory things at his body.

"I-I-I'm sorry, I—" he stammered at last, sitting up quickly. "I hope I didn't—um . . . "

"Is anyone hurt?" said Ms. Snapper, standing up and

looking over the bus, row by row. "Everybody okay?" Once she had seen that nobody in class had been hurt by the bus's sudden halt, she turned back to the bus driver. "What happened??"

"Something's on the windshield!" said the gray-haired man. He had pulled the bus to the side of the road. "Biggest insect I've ever seen!"

All the students craned their heads to look. There was a large, pinkish object slowly sliding down the windshield. It was the size of a lapdog, or a fat cat, or . . .

"FP?" Fisher said in disbelief. He popped up and bolted toward the front of the bus. "I, um, I'm sorry, Ms. Snapper. That's my pig." Ms. Snapper and the driver looked at him like he had a marmoset tap-dancing on his head.

"Why is your—um, *pig*—on the front of our bus?" Ms. Snapper turned back to stare at FP, who had now slid down to the bottom of the windshield.

"I honestly wish I knew," Fisher said. "I'll go get him."

Fisher hopped out of the passenger door just as FP slipped off the bottom of the windshield, leaving a thin, translucent streak behind him. Mr. Bas's hair gel! He must have been glued to the top of the bus this whole time, though how he had ended up there was a mystery. It looked like the effects of the hair gel were finally wearing off.

Fisher caught the very tired-looking pig in his arms.

"Are you all right, boy?" Fisher asked. FP looked up and snorted at Fisher before nuzzling his chest. "You just don't like to be left behind, do you?"

Fisher carried FP back onto the bus. All the kids burst into a chorus of "aww" and "Let me see him! Let me see him!"

Ms. Snapper looked down at FP, who looked back at her and snuffled piteously. She tentatively reached a hand down and scratched his head, and he made a low contented sound.

"Well . . ." she said doubtfully, "I can't imagine how he got up there, but we're more than halfway to LA by now. As long as you can keep him under control, he can come along."

Fisher bit his lip to keep from saying that keeping FP under control was like trying to lasso an eel. He simply nodded and forced a smile, and carried FP back to Veronica's seat. FP seemed to remember Veronica because as soon as Fisher sat down, the little pig tapped her with a front hoof and nuzzled his snout into her side.

"Oh," she said, smiling a bit forcedly. "Hi, FP."

"So," Fisher said, wishing he had thought to use the CONVERSATIONAL TOPICS function on his watch before now.

Before Fisher could get another word out, FP leapt out of his arms and into Veronica's lap. She gave a surprised squeal as he began chewing her hair. Then he found her purse strap, which he obviously thought would be delicious. He clamped his mouth down around it like a dog with a bone.

"FP!" Fisher said, trying to pry his pet off her bag. Veronica managed to remove the pig's jaws, stifling a frustrated sigh.

"Fisher, if it's all right, I'd like to just listen to music for a while. Besides, you should go back to your seat before Ms. Snapper catches you."

Fisher smiled weakly, feeling his heart freeze into a solid ball and drop into his stomach with a splash.

Fisher glanced out the window as he made his way back to his seat and did a triple take.

The car—that same car—was still behind them and had pulled to the shoulder when the bus had stopped. Black as a crow in a tar pit and just as creepy. As the bus pulled back onto the highway, so did the car, careful to maintain its distance. Then a truck blocked Fisher's line of sight for a moment and when it had passed, the car was gone.

"So *there* you are," said Amanda as Fisher inched as far down in his seat as he could. "Are you going to help me or what?"

"How about this?" he mumbled, half to himself. "I'll just go live in a cave somewhere and let Two be the only Fisher."

Amanda quirked an eyebrow as though considering it.

Then she shook her head. "No way," she said. "I'm not sneaking into some cave to bring you food. Come on, let's focus."

FP curled up in Fisher's lap and went to sleep. Fisher leaned back in his seat, wishing he could go to sleep, too—possibly forever.

≋ CHAPTER 5 ≋

I made Two so I could use him to take attention away from me. It's been sort of like using an anchor as a paperweight. —Fisher Bas, *Extended Clone Log*

The bus was at last making its way into the outskirts of Los Angeles. Trevor, who suffered from intense motion sickness, had made two more hurried runs to the bathroom. Spitballs papered the bus like a newly fallen snow. The documentary was finally over.

As they approached LA proper, the land, the air, and even the light seemed to change. A weird, faintly orange glow was pulsing out from the city like it was powered by ancient and terrible magic.

"This place looks a lot bigger in person," Amanda said, gaping out the window.

Fisher could only nod, awestruck. The city stretched vastly alongside the massive highways, which criss-crossed the landscape like angry concrete fingers. FP struggled up and worked his way onto Amanda's lap to get a better view. She didn't seem to notice. The down-town loomed in the distance, skyscrapers clustering together like points on a crown.

51

"We only have a couple days," Amanda said, half in a daze. "Where do we even begin?"

The black car had vanished. Fisher had tried to keep track of it during the trip, but he hadn't spotted it out of any windows for almost two hours. Maybe it was gone.

"Welcome to LA!" Ms. Snapper stood up, wobbling a bit. "The city of dreams! "

Fisher felt a stony mass of doubt begin to pile onto his shoulders. The city was huge and sprawling, and contained millions of people—and he needed to find exactly one of them. At this point, there were only two things he could count on: Amanda's relentless, single-minded determination, and Two's ability to cause chaos and draw attention to himself.

An hour later, the bus rolled to a stop next to a large complex of film lots. The studio buildings were huge, cement-walled monoliths, like giant warehouses set in the middle a perfectly laid grid of asphalt pathways. Everyone started babbling excitedly about the stars they might see, films that were in production, and whether any of the movies might need extras.

"All right, everyone off, quickly and quietly. Form a line next to the bus," Ms. Snapper said. The other chaperones, who had buried themselves in books and headphones during the trip, stood up. They counted heads and checked attendance as the kids filed off. Fisher carried FP off the bus, and set the little pig down at his heels.

"Now you stay by me, okay, boy?" Fisher said sternly. FP looked up and blinked, looking like he hadn't quite understood. "I have food for you if you do." FP squealed happily and brushed up against Fisher's leg. Fisher didn't actually have any food for FP, since he hadn't planned on FP's presence, but he figured he could dig some up later. The *only* way to get his flying friend to behave was the promise of a treat.

The class lined up by the bus, which had pulled up right next to a white-walled studio building. After a minute, a small door opened in its side and a tall, black-haired woman in a dark, sleek-fitting business suit emerged, a close-lipped smile on her face.

"On behalf of *Strange Science*," she said in a smooth voice, "I would like to welcome you to Los Angeles. My name is Lucy Fir, personal assistant to Dr. Devilish. I'll be your guide today, and I'll do my best to answer any questions you may have. Oh, look! Here comes the doctor himself."

Everyone turned to look. Dr. Devilish stepped out of the building, trailed by several staff members. He was even taller than he looked on TV, and just as good-looking, with slicked-back black hair and a thin, precisely trimmed goatee. His glaringly white teeth contrasted with his perfectly uniform almond-hued tan.

Ms. Snapper turned to face him. Her smile was so large it seemed to be consuming her face.

"Oh, Dr. Devilish!" she said, her voice quavering slightly. "We weren't expecting to see you so soon. It's a great pleasure . . . really, an honor, I mean. . . ." A reddish glow started at the base of her neck and quickly spread to her cheeks.

"Hmm?" Dr. Devilish said with a start, as though seeing them for the first time. Then he flashed them a dazzling smile. "Oh, yes, the students. Welcome to the show! I'll be with you in a little while. I just have some . . . *catalysts* to sequence. If you'll excuse me."

"Well, all right, I suppose. . . ." Ms. Snapper said, obviously crestfallen. "But we'll see you soon. Very soon." He didn't seem to take much notice of the bright smile that she projected at him as he turned away. Amanda turned to Fisher and raised an eyebrow. He shrugged in response.

Dr. Devilish headed for a group of trailers huddled together across the studio lot. Lucy turned to speak to one of his other assistants, and Amanda took the opportunity to break away from the group and catch up with Dr. Devilish, holding out a pen and her notebook. He looked down with a tired smile, and after exchanging a few words with

Theories on what
Dr. Devilish could really be:
(because no scientist looks that good)

secretly is Vic Daring
an alien
an android
a hologram
*this entire trip is a bad dream
   -or- virtual reality simulation
a mass hallucination?

Amanda, took the pen and scribbled a quick note.

She rejoined the class as Ms. Fir began the tour and fell into step beside Fisher. Fisher caught a glimpse of Amanda's open notebook, with the page that Dr. Devilish had written on. It said *To Sandra*, followed by an autograph in elaborate script with the final *h* trailing off into a pointed tail.

"Who's Sandra?" Fisher said, raising an eyebrow.

"He must have misheard me when I told him my name," Amanda said dejectedly.

The studios looked more or less identical from the outside: squat, gray, and very long. Lucy Fir led the class along a broad width of pavement between two studios.

Technicians, production assistants, lighting and sound technicians, and other film workers hurried past them carrying equipment, papers, and coffee, or navigated the lots in small golf carts.

"It's amazing who you'll see around here on an ordinary day," Lucy said, walking confidently backward between the two studio buildings. "Actors, directors, legendary producers . . . Just one lot over is where *Keel Me Now* is being filmed, with Kevin Keels. . . . Oh!" Lucy laughed. "Speak of the devil. Or I should say—the hero."

The class had just rounded the corner of the building. There, in a denim jacket and mirrored sunglasses, standing all of five foot two, was Kevin Keels. A gaggle of assistants, bodyguards, and helpers swarmed around him.

Instantly, the class went crazy.

Everyone shouted, screamed, or shrieked at Keels as he strutted past them, and he waved to everyone with his usual casual confidence.

Then something strange happened. When he saw Fisher, he paused, lowered his shades, and waved before walking on.

The whole class fell abruptly into silence. Veronica was staring at Fisher with her mouth hanging open. Fisher tried to say something, but all that emerged was an *errrrghhh* sound.

"All right, kids. Let's keep the tour moving!" Lucy Fir

gestured for the students to follow her.

Fisher tried to ignore the fact that the other kids were still whispering and stealing glances at him.

"Wow, Fisher," Veronica whispered, gazing at him with newfound admiration. "Did Kevin Keels really just wave at you?"

"Um . . . I think he was just, y'know, saying hello to the class." Fisher pulled at his collar. Keels had looked directly at him when he waved. There was no doubt about it: he recognized Fisher. Or at least, he recognized Two. Two's video must really be making the rounds.

"It sure looked like it," Veronica said, gazing after the pop singer like a trail of gold coins was falling out of his socks.

He sighed. Fisher felt like his insides were trapped in a vortex of spiraling arctic wind. One thing was certain; the value of K was skyrocketing. At this rate, his first chance to kiss Veronica might be when their fossils were put on display.

≋ CHAPTER 6 ≋

I see why they call them stars. Groups of smaller people orbit around them, and most of them are a lot harder to look at up close.

—Two, Personal Journal

Fisher's brain was working furiously as Lucy Fir led the class toward the entrance to one of the studios. Kevin Keels—one of the most famous people in the world—had recognized him! It was incredible.

And very, very bad.

FP's insistent snout-bumping was starting to make his ankle sore. "Yes, boy, I know you're hungry," Fisher whispered as FP began to gnaw on his sneaker. "As soon as we finish this tour I'll find you something to eat, I promise."

"And now, we'll have a look at the *Strange Science* set," said Lucy, leading the class through the door.

They passed inside the vast, white building, and there was a collective gasp as the students recognized the set of *Strange Science* and took in the dozens of cameras and boom mics littering the space.

Production crew members hurried back and forth getting the set ready for the next episode's taping. Camera crews were adjusting and calibrating their instruments, set workers were placing props and equipment, and they were all being followed around by assistants holding clipboards, calculators, and coffee cups big enough to double as hats.

Set against one wall was the craft services table, a wide, foldout table with a spread of rolls, fruit, cold cuts, and a variety of snacks for the cast and crew. Small groups congregated around it, piling food on their plates and discussing filming and design decisions. FP started to veer toward the table like it was a giant electromagnet, and he had a horseshoe tied to his head. Fisher gently steered him away with little taps of his foot.

"Not now, boy," he said. "I'll get you something in a minute."

"Over here is Dr. Devilish's main worktable," Ms. Fir went on, "which I'm sure you'll recognize if you've seen the show." The table was eight feet wide and made of shining chrome, equipped with a variety of apparatus, including two sinks, multiple clamps, air hoses, and built-in test-tube racks. Hanging above it on flexible metal arms were three ceiling-mounted microscopes.

Fisher took a deep breath as he looked over the marvelous machinery. There was nothing quite like the sight of gleaming, cutting-edge apparatus to ease his mind and remind him of home.

"Over here is Dr. Devilish's personal barbatic-aesthetic automaton," Ms. Fir said, pointing to a small machine sprouting several multi-jointed arms sitting on a tall stand.

"His what?" said Ben Kraus, a tall, spindly boy with a spiked-up haircut.

"His beard-trimming robot," she clarified.

Amanda was barely paying attention to the tour. Fisher, in spite of his fascination with Dr. Devilish and his show, found focusing on the tour difficult. He had a couple of days to find Two and as powerful as his mind was, he hadn't come up with much of a coherent plan.

"Hey, could somebody give me a hand with this boom? It's got a loose clasp."

Fisher turned around.

A technician with close-cropped blond hair was standing behind him, holding a long, black steel boom with a foam oval enclosing the microphone at its tip. The clasp securing its extendable section was broken.

Fisher studied the boom for a second.

"I have an idea," he said.

The man fiddled exasperatedly with the broken clasp, struggling to keep the extendable handle from slipping from his grasp. "Knock yourself out."

"Have you got a cloth or a rag on you?" Fisher asked.

The man pulled a cleaning cloth out of his back pocket

and passed it to Fisher with one hand.

Fisher bent over and began to rub FP's back with the cloth, which made FP promptly fall asleep. After a few moments, the last dregs of the highly adhesive hair gel in FP's system were worked out of his skin, and Fisher stepped up to the boom, the cloth tacky in his hands.

Fisher wrung the cloth around the extending joint, and in short order the joint was sealed up with the stuff. The technician tested it. His face broke into a grin.

"Thanks for the help!" he said. "I do sound around here, and whatever else they can stick me with. My name's Henry." He extended his hand.

"Fisher," Fisher said as his hand was engulfed by Henry's.

"I'd be interested to hear about what exactly you just did. For now I've got to get to work, though. Thanks again!"

Henry walked away, and Fisher smiled a bit to himself. It felt good to be appreciated for something small. It was a good middle ground between being completely ignored and being celebrated as a conquering hero.

Then, out of the corner of his eye, he spotted a tall man wearing a dark suit, watching Fisher with a severe look on his face. When he realized Fisher had seen him, he gave a friendly half smile and backed into a dark corner.

Probably just an executive, Fisher thought.

Alternate uses for Dad's hair gel:

allows spies to climb the
sides of buildings
fix the space shuttle
styling for hair-metal bands
cleaning the floor (instead of
mopping, put down a layer
and peel it up)

Probably.

There was a tremendous, clattering crash, and thoughts of the man in the suit flew out of Fisher's mind.

"Hey!" a man shouted. "Who let this animal in here??"

Oh, no. Too late, Fisher realized FP was gone.

He turned around: the craft services table had been toppled by his determined and very hungry flying pig. Kaiser rolls rolled away in all directions, cheese slices lay haphazardly everywhere, gallons of water and lemonade seeped across the floor, and FP was wearing a cold-cut sombrero. From a distance, it looked like a piece of turkey.

"Will somebody get this *pig* out of here?" a red-faced production assistant was trying to mop up the spilled drinks.

"I'm sorry," Fisher said, hurrying forward, "I'm sorry, he's just—"

"Brilliant!" a trumpeting voice cut in. As Fisher scooped FP into his arms, he saw a tall woman wearing a bright green suit, and a pair of enormous sunglasses that made her look like an insect. Her teeth looked like they were made of imported marble and were polished every hour on the hour. "Kevin told me that you were here, Basley. I'm glad I caught you! I knew that *you* had enormous potential, but I had no idea you had an animal sidekick! Did you see how he swooped into the table leg? I swear, he actually flew!"

"Uh . . ." Fisher said, looking around as he realized that everyone in the class was staring at him. Who was Basley?

"Just imagine the possibilities!" the woman said, looking majestically into the distance, which in this case was a wall ten feet in front of her face.

"The possibilities for what?" Fisher said, dreading the answer.

"Commercials! Public service announcements! Maybe even a television series!" she proclaimed, walking up and scratching FP on the back as he ate the turkey off the top of his own head. "A pig with his talent could go far. Very, very far! I insist we have a meeting to discuss it!"

"Well," Fisher said, "I guess, uh . . ."

"And maybe we can talk about your own career possibilities, Basley," she said, giving a wink that Fisher could barely see under her titanic sunglasses. "I know that you've been in contact with that Lulu O'Lunney, but she can't hold a candle to me. O'Lunney couldn't agent her way out of a cardboard box! A potential star should be served by a star! My card." She handed Fisher a business card that read in a giant, blocky font, GG MCGEE, and below that, AGENT OF STARS.

"Um, okay, yeah, whatever," Fisher said, desperate to end the conversation.

"Perfect!" McGee said. "Bring him by tomorrow at three thirty, and we'll talk."

"Tomorrow's Saturday," Fisher pointed out.

"Time is money!" GG barked out. She clapped Fisher on the shoulder. "I'll see you tomorrow!" Then she winked at FP. "Fame and glory await you, my little pink friend."

Fisher looked down at FP as GG McGee walked away. He tried to look as stern as possible. "What have you gotten me into now, boy? If you could go fifteen minutes without a snack . . ."

"What was that all about, Fisher?" Ms. Snapper asked.

Fisher shoved his hands in his pockets. He had been in LA for less than an hour, and already Two's growing popularity was proving disastrous.

"Yes, uh, Basley's my stage name." Fisher forced a big grin onto his face and avoided Amanda's eyes. "I made a little tape and some talent scouts must have seen it. But for now, I really want to focus on schoolwork," Fisher hurried to add. "Just, you know, being a normal kid and everything."

"Cool!" Veronica said, turning her beautiful smile on him. The light of that smile warmed him up from his head to his feet. "So Kevin really *was* waving to you!" she continued, even more excitedly.

"Uh . . . yeah, I guess so," Fisher said as the warmth became a harsh sunburn.

As the tour resumed, Amanda turned to glower at him. "Listen, Fisher Bas!" she hissed, tugging Fisher away from the other students. "I don't know what game you think you're playing, but we're here to find Two, not chase flying-pig movie dreams."

"Look," Fisher said, "That woman—GG—has clearly heard of Two. She might be able to help us find him."

"Fine," Amanda said, putting her hands on her hips. "But I'm going with you to the meeting, and *I'm* doing the talking. Congratulations, *Basley*, you've just hired your first manager." She extended her right hand. Fisher knew there was no point in arguing, so he allowed her to crush his hand. Again.

Less than an hour in Hollywood, and things had gone from bad to terrible.

≋ CHAPTER 7 ≋

There are three kinds of people in the world: People who cause problems, people who solve problems, and people who sit in comfortable interview chairs saying things about problems and getting paid a lot of money.

—Dr. Devilish, TV Interview

"Rat! There's a *rat* in the door!"

The arrival at the King of Hollywood hotel wasn't going quite as smoothly as planned. Fisher scanned the lobby and felt his blood drain all the way to his toes. Not *again*. FP was stuck inside the revolving glass front doors. He must have wandered after someone and gotten trapped.

The original King of Hollywood location had started out looking like any other fast-food place, but as the chain had taken off, it had grown to monstrous size. Now, in addition to the expanded, well-decorated restaurant on the ground floor, a twenty-story hotel soared into the sky. It was an upscale, classy establishment. And not one that Fisher imagined would be welcoming to pigs, even small, flying ones.

An old woman, wearing a satin evening dress, a string

of ping-pong-sized pearls, and spectacles with lenses so thick they would probably stop bullets, continued screaming and pointing. Fisher was barely able to rotate the door back and scoop FP out before several of the hotel staff descended upon them.

"He's not a rat!" Fisher protested. "He's not a rat! He's a little pig, and he's fully house trained." *Other than his tendency to stalk people and leap onto buses,* Fisher thought, but they didn't need to know that.

"I'm sorry, young man," said a woman, whose name tag identified her as the manager, "but I'm afraid we do not allow pets of any kind in this establishment." She sniffed in distaste as she looked down at FP. "*Particularly* not pigs."

"But—" Fisher started to protest.

"No exceptions," she said sternly. "Now get that thing out of here, before I bring him to the fryer myself."

Fisher stalked out of the hotel with FP in his arms, fuming. Amanda and Veronica followed him out.

"What are we supposed to do now?" Amanda whispered fiercely. "Your stupid pig is going to mess up our whole plan to find . . ." She trailed off when she realized Veronica was right behind her. She settled for crossing her arms and frowning.

"I'm really sorry, Fisher," Veronica said. "Maybe we

Official Operating Hours
Original King of Hollywood Restaurant
at the King of Hollywood Hotel

MONDAY–FRIDAY 6:30am–10pm

SATURDAY 6:30am–12am

SUNDAY 6:30am–9pm

potential times to sneak into kitchen
and find secret special sauce recipe
Friday after closing, Saturday morning rush?

can rig up a bed for FP on the bus. He'll be happy there, won't he?"

"Maybe." He didn't add: *when FP really does fly.* He headed dejectedly toward the tour bus, trying to calculate the odds that FP would be content to sleep on the bus without chewing through all of the seat cushions—and possibly the engine cables—in protest.

Trevor Weiss was tugging his oversized suitcase with all of his strength, still trying to wrestle it out of the luggage compartment. A final yank sent Trevor rolling backward onto the ground. The suitcase sprang open, and its contents tumbled onto the pavement: some clothes, a small blanket, and a metal contraption that looked like a miniature instrument of torture.

"What's this?" Fisher said, picking up the little blanket.

"My feet get cold, so I always carry an extra blanket," Trevor explained, pulling himself to his feet unsteadily.

"And the other thing?" Fisher said. "What *is* that?"

"Orthodontic stuff," Trevor said. "I'm supposed to hook it to my braces when I sleep."

Fisher looked back and forth between the blanket and the headgear and the pig. And he had an idea.

"May I borrow those?" Fisher asked Trevor, indicating the two items. Trevor shrugged and nodded, curious, and Fisher deftly wrapped FP up in the blanket so that only a small part of his head was visible. Then he wrestled the headgear onto FP's head, pinning down the pig's ears. FP squirmed and honked a little in protest, but ultimately relented.

"Voilà!" Fisher said triumphantly. Amanda recoiled. Veronica giggled.

Fisher had succeeded in making FP resemble a very, very unattractive baby.

He tucked FP into his arms and strolled back through

the lobby, whistling loudly and trying to look casual.

A young couple strolled up to Fisher and looked down at FP.

"Oh, hello there!" said the tall young woman, waving at the sleeping pig. "Is that your little brother?"

"Er, yeah, that's right," Fisher said. "His name is FP. That's, um, short for . . . Frederick Percival."

"Sounds very noble," said the man, adjusting his glasses. They both bent down to take a closer look.

"Gee, he's got such a . . . distinctive face. Don't you agree, sweetie?" the woman said with a forced smile.

"Oh, yes," the man choked out. "Very distinctive." He cleared his throat. "Well, have a good day."

"You too," Fisher said as they walked away, before letting out a sigh of relief.

Fisher found the rest of the class already seated in the restaurant's massive dining room, sat down, and set FP in his lap. The blanket seemed to have a tranquilizing effect on him, and Fisher listened for FP's light snoring, to make sure the little pig didn't suffocate under all the headgear.

Veronica plopped down next to him.

"Sheesh. This trip has hardly begun and it's already crazy," she said.

"Y-yes, crazy it has, uh, been," Fisher said. Veronica's elbow was touching his, and a feeling of numbness crept into his mouth, as though he'd just been shot with Novocain. He gestured to the sleeping pig in his arms. "He definitely . . . superbly . . . he's trouble."

"At least he's cute," Veronica said, smiling down at the odd bundle in Fisher's lap. "So . . . did you *really* submit a taped audition to a studio?"

"I . . . did, yes," Fisher said. The pang hit him like a club right to the middle of his chest. More lies. Always more lies. Two had done something great, something that excited Veronica. Something that *he* could never do.

He had made Two so that the clone would pretend to be him. Now the only thing that would hold anyone's attention was pretending to be Two.

Veronica's eyes were shining; he had to *keep* them shining, even if it did mean using Two for his own personal gain. "It was . . . kind of unplanned. I'm not sure whether I'll really be pursuing the Hollywood thing, but I'm keeping my options open."

"That's great," Veronica said. "I'll have to . . . ooh, hang on a second."

She whipped around toward one of the restaurant's many TVs, which had just started playing the music video for the latest Kevin Keels hit, "Gift-Wrapped Heart (Please Don't Tear the Paper)." Fisher sank a little farther into his seat.

He dug into the middle of a mountain of Monarch-sized

star fries, and something brushed his finger. He thought
maybe a napkin had mistakenly been put on the plate, but
when he moved a few fries aside, he realized it was a note.
He fought back his instinctive reaction with an enormous
effort and went on eating, on autopilot, the brief message
burned into his mind.

I'VE GOT MY EYE ON
YOU, FISHER. OR SHOULD
I SAY . . . FISHERS?

≋ CHAPTER 8 ≋

All the studying and learning on earth won't stop the surge of instinct that pops up when you realize you're being hunted. Of course this doesn't mean you'll be able to run any faster.

—Fisher Bas, Personal Notes

Wham. Wham. Wham. WHAM. WHAM.

Amanda opened her hotel room door to Fisher's frantic knocking.

"Fisher? What's going on?"

"Someone is on to me," Fisher whispered. "I got a note. Someone knows about Two."

"Who do you think it could be?" she said, looking over her shoulder to make sure her roommate was still in the shower.

"I'm not sure, but . . ." He gulped, and leaned even closer to Amanda. "I'm pretty sure we're being followed."

"Followed?" Amanda parroted, her familiar steely frown returning. "Is there something you haven't told me?"

Fisher put his forehead in his hand, sighing through clenched teeth. "The government agency my mother was working for shut down the AGH project and confiscated all samples. They know some AGH is missing, and I think they suspect I took it."

"And it didn't occur to you to tell me this *particular* part of the story?" she said.

"I didn't find out until we'd already made our plan. And I didn't think I was even a suspect until today. Besides, I didn't want to get *you* into trouble, on top of everything else."

Amanda exhaled. "Well," she said, "the only thing for us to do is stick to the plan. Go to the meeting with GG McGee, try and find Two from there, and get to him as fast as we can. I trust you'll figure out a way to deal with the spies by the time we do. You escaped from TechX. How hard can dealing with a couple of government agents be?"

"Right," Fisher said, picturing himself handcuffed to a steel chair in a windowless room.

When he returned to his room, the TV was on, and Warren, his roommate, was sitting on his bed, bouncing slightly.

"What's on?" Fisher said. He wanted desperately to distract himself from his growing sense of peril.

"It's a preview of *Sci-Fi: Survivor!*" Warren said cheerfully. "They're talking about the maze, and the challenges contestants will have to face."

The camera was sweeping dramatically over a some-what cartoonish landscape. There were prehistoric-looking jungles of plastic and gauzy foam, with narrow walkways stretched across bubbling water that was prob-ably about the temperature of a comfortable hot tub. Ani-matronic dinosaurs plodded clumsily around, swinging rubbery claws and tails. Other parts of the maze were more futuristic and were populated by shining robots that shot foam darts from rotating barrels in their chests.

"Looks fun," said Fisher, smiling weakly. He would almost rather be chased by *real* dinosaurs than be in the position he was in now.

"Sure does!" said Warren. "I can't wait for it to pre-miere next week! Well, time for bed." He clicked the TV off with the remote and literally passed out sitting up, his unconscious body slowly falling back against the pillows.

Fisher sighed and climbed into bed next to the already-sleeping FP, wishing sleep would come to him as quickly as it did for Warren. It was going to be a long night of staring at the clock.

On Saturday morning, during the tour of Hollywood Bou-levard, Fisher's heart jumped every time he spotted some-one in a suit and sunglasses. Unfortunately, in downtown LA, that description covered a lot of people. The city was bathed in bright sunlight, keeping the air at an exact 73 degrees, and the Hollywood sign loomed on a hill in the distance, gleaming in the sun, but Fisher couldn't enjoy any of it.

Spies seemed to be lurking everywhere, as they had once again in his nightmares. The massive sandstone-block courtyard of the Egyptian Theatre offered plenty of hiding places with its thick hieroglyph-painted columns and pharaoh-head statues. The El Capitan Theatre's marquee, made of shimmering gold trim and flickering lightbulbs, made him think of a thousand watchful eyes. Happy tourists babbled in dozens of languages, and almost all of them had cameras. He felt like every lens was trained on him.

Fisher pulled a tiny spray can from his pocket that was marked with a generic antimosquito label. Its actual properties made light reflect off him in such a way that a camera trying to capture his image would record only a bright yellow blur. He had originally developed the technology—as he did most of his inventions—as a defense against the Vikings' harassment. Every year on school picture day, the Vikings found some new way to humiliate Fisher. Once they'd stolen a vial of squid ink from the bio lab and flung it all over his shirt. Once they'd stolen the cafeteria's vat of homemade hoisin sauce, which had been known to permanently stain bricks, and upended it over Fisher's head. It hadn't taken long for Fisher to decide that he'd rather have no picture at all than one the Vikings insisted on destroying.

He sprayed it all around himself until he nearly choked on it. One of his classmates gave him a strange look.

"Sunscreen," Fisher said with a nervous laugh.

Fisher kept his arms locked tightly around FP. The unfamiliar sights, smells, and sounds gave FP the nervous, destructive instincts of a caffeinated hyena. He couldn't afford to let FP get away when a single wrong turn could land him in the hands of the FBI or the CIA or someone with even scarier initials.

The Walk of Fame stretched before them, the highly polished black stone decorated with rows and rows of rose-colored marble stars, each bearing the name of a director, actor, or other famous film industry professional in polished brass. People began pointing out their favorite stars and posing for pictures, joining all of the other tourists from across the globe in the excited shuffle.

It was almost lunchtime. Fisher had only a few hours before his meeting with GG McGee, Agent of Stars—his best shot at finding Two. And he still had no idea how he would get away from Ms. Snapper.

The Chinese Theatre came into view. Warren started running in crazy loop de loops around the ornamental pillars that flanked the entrance to its main courtyard. As the class came to a stop, Fisher glanced at the street traffic, and his shoulders seized up as an awfully familiar-looking black car came into view. He looked around for a spot to hide himself when he heard a collective gasp from nearby, and turned just in time to see a gang of seven girls who looked about fourteen descend upon him.

"Basley!" one of them said.

"Basley!" echoed her companions in eerily identical voices.

"Can we have your autograph?"

"Oh my God! You're even cuter in real life!"

Fisher was suddenly lost in a whirlpool of perfect tans and bleached white-blond hair. He could hardly tell where one of them ended and the other began. The girls blurred together into a many-headed beast as Fisher tried to free one hand for a pen. One of them noticed FP.

"Oh my god!" she squealed. "Is this your baby brother or sister?"

"Yes," Fisher said, half in a daze, "he's my brother."

"Awwwwww!" they said in disturbing unison. They bent down to get a closer look at the "baby."

"Oh . . . gee," one said, as she got a closer look. "He's very, um . . ."

"Pink and healthy-looking," another chimed in quickly.

"What's his name?" one said.

"FP," Fisher said, trying to remember what he'd told

the last people who'd asked. "It stands for . . . Frankie Philip."

"Ohhh, hi, Frankie!" another one said, waving at FP, who was starting to stir, and looking around in confusion.

"Hey!" another voice cut in. "I think Kevin Keels just walked into the theatre!"

Like a flock of pigeons being charged by a small child, the girls exploded into motion, leaving nothing but a dizzy Fisher and a cloud of hair-spray fumes in their wake.

Fisher shook his head, trying to clear it. FP blinked at him confusedly. The black car was gone. He didn't know if its occupants had seen him or not, but with any luck the giggly wall that had just surrounded him had done the trick.

Did those girls really just call him *cute*?

Fisher looked up and saw Veronica. She winked at him. "I didn't really see Kevin," she said, and he realized that she was the one who had shouted.

"Thank you," Fisher said fervently. Veronica smiled at him. He felt like the already bright sun had been dialed up and focused just a little bit right around him.

As Veronica turned back to admire the architecture, Fisher felt hands gripping his shoulders. Before he could shout, he was spun around on his heels.

"If you're not too busy with your *adoring fans*," Amanda

Practice Basley Signatures
in case of girl mob emergency

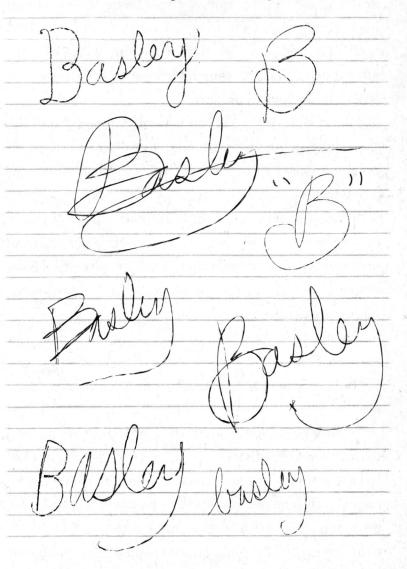

said, her hands on her hips, "we've got work to get done."

"There are other ways to get my attention besides grabbing me," Fisher said, without bothering to conceal his irritation.

She ignored him. "We have a meeting with GG right after lunch," she said, tapping her watch. "That gives us less than an hour to prepare."

Fisher sighed. "I don't see how we can do it," he said. "Ms. Snapper has been keeping a really careful eye on everyone since FP's incident at the hotel. How are we supposed to get away?"

"Like this," Amanda said, holding up a piece of paper. It was the sheet of notebook paper that she'd had Dr. Devilish sign. Fisher saw that in between the phrase *To Sandra* and his signature, Amanda had written: *I need to see you. Alone. 3 P.M.*

"He didn't mishear me," Amanda smirked. "I told him to write 'Sandra.'"

"But . . ." Fisher said, and then it dawned on him. "Sandra . . ."

". . . Snapper," Amanda finished, adjusting her glasses to emphasize her raised eyebrow. "Sandra's her first name. In case you haven't noticed, our teacher turns into a fire-engine-red wobbly-kneed wonder anytime Dr. Devilish is even mentioned. We'll be going back to the hotel for lunch soon. I'm going to slip this into her purse as we walk into the restaurant. If this works, she'll find it before we're done."

Fisher was speechless for a moment. Amanda never let anything keep her from getting what she wanted, but this was an impressive scheme even by her standards.

He didn't like the idea of lying to his teacher, but this small deception was nothing compared to the massive lie he'd been frantically spinning ever since Two had come into being.

"All right," he said. "Let's do it. With any luck we'll get one step closer to Two." He just had to hope that Two's next step didn't take him right into the spotlight.

≋ CHAPTER 9 ≋

Step one: have talent.
Step two: get hired.
Most people skip step one. It's not as important.

—*GG McGee*

In the fifteen minutes it took to get the class off the bus and assembled for lunch, Fisher let FP run around like crazy in the grass next to the parking lot. Now, thankfully, the pig was calm again, and he lay in Fisher's lap, accepting the bits and pieces of special sauce–coated French fries that Fisher periodically handed down to him.

Some of the kids were showing each other photos they'd taken in front of the sidewalk stars, and many were still buzzing about having run into Kevin Keels at the *Strange Science* studio lot the day before. Fisher kept having the uncomfortable feeling that people were talking about him, too.

Or rather—that people were talking about "Basley."

Fisher couldn't believe that Two had already catapulted himself into the limelight with a single audition tape. As much as he'd marveled at Two's ability to attain instant popularity at school, it seemed that he'd underestimated just how charismatic the clone could be.

"Fisher," Amanda whispered, and pointed subtly. Ms. Snapper had just come out of the restroom, looking flustered. Her cheeks had turned a strawberry shade, and she was adjusting her hair obsessively with one hand while clutching a folded-up piece of paper in the other. Amanda's note. She had dropped it casually in Ms. Snapper's handbag as they filed into the restaurant; obviously, it had found its target.

"Boys and girls," she said, reaching the middle of the big table and taking a deep breath to compose herself. "There's been a . . . minor schedule change, due to some . . . business—important business!—that I have to attend to. I'm giving you the rest of the afternoon off."

The table erupted in cheers. Ms. Snapper held up a hand to silence the class. "You'll have to stay on the hotel grounds, but you can use the pool or the other facilities if you wish. Mr. Crenshaw?"

The reedy, bespectacled assistant librarian who had filled the last chaperone spot walked up to Ms. Snapper, paper napkin still tucked into his shirt collar.

"Yes, ma'am?" he said.

"You're in charge while I'm away," she said, and ignoring Mr. Crenshaw's stammering protests, turned and

85

practically sprinted from the restaurant.

Amanda looked at Fisher with a self-satisfied smirk on her face.

"We'll wait until people start to leave, and we'll slip out during the commotion," she said. "Crenshaw won't even notice. Yesterday he called me Penelope."

"Where did you learn how to be this devious?" Fisher asked, popping his last star fry into his mouth.

"It comes naturally," she replied with a grin.

At the end of lunch, Mr. Crenshaw attempted to round up the class.

"So, if everyone could just . . . if, perhaps, you could arrange yourselves in an orderly line . . ." Mr. Crenshaw spoke in a stuttering whisper. He darted from one table to another, making little brushing motions with his arms as if the students were dust motes he was trying to make float away. "P-please . . . if you could all just cooperate . . ."

"Now's our chance," Amanda whispered, once Mr. Crenshaw was busy at the next table. "Follow me." She slipped out of the group, Fisher following close behind, gripping FP tightly in Trevor's blanket. Fisher stole a glance back as they slipped out a side door. Crenshaw was frowning at the spot that Fisher and Amanda had just vacated. But just then, a star fry smacked Crenshaw in the back of his bald head, and a table of boys burst into laughter.

Fisher watched as Mr. Crenshaw swiveled around to lecture them.

They left the hotel, and Amanda hailed a cab with a two-finger whistle that made Fisher's teeth buzz. She gave the driver GG McGee's address, and off they went, careening onto a massive six-lane highway and zigzagging through the lanes with such speed, Fisher felt his brain rattling in his skull. Thankfully, the office was only a few minutes' drive away, and soon they were zipping off the highway and pulling up to GG's office.

The building where GG McGee worked was a swooping granite-and-glass monster, its front courtyard decorated with a statue that might have been a mythological figure—or an enormous centipede. It was difficult to tell. A flood of very important-looking men and women in very expensive, well-tailored suits went to and from the office, each talking into several electronic devices at once and wielding enough coffee to flood a living room.

In the elevator, Fisher and Amanda were nearly suffocated by a powerful fog of perfumes and colognes. When they reached the thirty-second floor, reeling from oxygen deprivation, they stumbled out into the plush hallway. The mahogany-paneled walls and ceiling were trimmed with silver. A circular black marble reception desk stood in the middle of a cluster of smaller corridors. The young woman behind the desk was unhurriedly tapping at a keyboard and looking very bored. The plate-glass window behind her desk was big enough to drive a train through, and Fisher felt himself sway dizzily just looking through it.

Fisher cleared his throat. "H-hello," he said as he approached the desk. Amanda hung back.

The receptionist looked up and glanced around, frowning. Then she raised her seat a little higher up, and saw Fisher, who was almost entirely dwarfed by her desk. She wrinkled her nose in distaste when she saw the strange-looking bundle in his arms.

"Can I help you?" she said in a tone suggesting that "yes" was the very last answer she wanted to hear.

"I'm here to see GG McGee," Fisher said, feeling very small and alone, especially since Amanda seemed to be having an attack of nerves. He shot her a glance over his shoulder and tried to give her a "get-over-here" look. "My name is Fish-uh, Basley."

The woman let out a long breath and tapped a key, looking over her screen for a moment.

"Fourth door on the right," she said, pointing to a corridor with a long, manicured finger.

"Thanks," Fisher croaked. He felt as though he'd just drunk a pint of sandpaper. He motioned to Amanda.

They advanced down the corridor, each step ringing hollowly on the polished marble.

"I'll be back," Amanda said as soon as they reached the

correct door. A huge placard read, in elaborate gold script, ***GG McGee.***

"Back?" Fisher spluttered. "Where are you going?"

"Just taking care of something quickly," she said. "Go on, I'll be right behind you."

Before Fisher could respond, Amanda slipped away. Part of him wanted to chase right after her. How could she run off on him at the last second, when she had insisted on coming in the first place? How did she expect him to do this on his own?

Thoughts whirled through his head, faster than his mom's gigantic centrifuge. He was posing as Two. So what would Two do? Two was brash, straightforward, fearless. He would walk right through that door without thinking twice.

He turned back toward the door, sucked in a deep breath, and knocked.

"Come in," he heard McGee's brassy voice proclaim. He turned the silver-plated knob, and walked in, FP cradled in one arm.

The office looked like the contents of a tourist-trap gift shop had been flung into a stateroom on the *Titanic*. Velvet-upholstered sofas accented with gold leaf were worn down to threads by piles of cheap plastic dolls, collectible drinking cups, and bags full of kazoos. An antique-looking grandfather clock with no hour hand stood in one corner, its brass pendulum being clung to by a stuffed monkey with Velcro paws.

GG sat behind a mahogany desk covered with bobbleheads and stacks of paper tall enough to cast long shadows. She wore a sharp-fitting gray suit and much more reasonable-looking sunglasses than the day before, although Fisher still didn't see why she was wearing them indoors. Her hair was coiffed into a perfect sweep.

"Basley!" she exclaimed, pointing to a leather-cushioned chair that looked like it could swallow him whole. "Come on in and have a seat. Is that our little star-to-be?" She looked at FP with a cheek-splitting grin.

"Hi, Ms. McGee," Fisher said, unwrapping FP's blanket and slipping off Trevor's headgear. "Yep, this is FP."

"Please, call me GG," McGee said, flipping through a binder on her desk. "Now, I've been working up some ideas for the little guy—what's his name again?"

"FP," Fisher repeated. "Flying Pig."

"I see," McGee said. "An adorable name for a personal pet, but we're going to need a stage name with a little more flash. What do you think of Jet Jowls, the Wonder Pig, or Ace McSnout?"

"Um . . ." Fisher said, looking down at FP.

"Too ordinary?" McGee tapped her chin. "Thinking of something more sophisticated? How about Ham-let, Prince of the Sky or Sir Flapsis Bacon?"

"Sir Flapsis isn't bad," Fisher admitted honestly.

"Well, we have plenty of time to make a final decision. Here are some ideas my team and I have been pitching back and forth. Picture it: a run-down old city full of crumbling buildings that are always catching fire. The fire department does the best it can, but they have trouble rescuing people trapped on the upper floors! So who do they send for? A humble pig gifted with the power of flight to swoop in and save the day! We'll call it *Out of the Flying Pan*."

FP had perked up in Fisher's lap. Noticing the large tray of baked goods on the desk, he began devouring bagels and muffins with astounding speed. GG either didn't mind or didn't notice.

"Or imagine him as a superhero!" she continued. "Similar setting, a town where crime is running out of control. The police are overwhelmed. Nobody can stem the tide. Nobody except . . . *The Pink Avenger*. He uses his powers of flight, his sensitive, crime-detecting ears, and his mighty snout to fight crime. Or we can go the holiday movie route! Imagine: it's days before Christmas and Dancer has a broken leg. How will Santa power his sleigh with only seven reindeer? But then, a lowly stable pig, the property of a poor elf farmer, accidentally falls out of the hayloft and realizes he can fly! The reindeer don't accept him at first, but eventually he warms everyone's hearts and fills in the eighth spot, and the sleigh can fly at last!"

She set down her sunglasses, revealing electric-green eyes, and whisked away a tear. She leaned across the desk and started to pet FP, who began to shudder uncomfortably in response.

"What a sweet little creature you are," she said, scratching at FP's ears. "You're going to have a marvelous future in—*oww*!!" As FP snapped at her, she yanked her hand back quickly. Suddenly, her face contorted in a frown, and she spat out: "Why, you miserable little bacon factory! I'll—" She caught herself quickly and immediately pasted a large, sugary smile back on her face. ". . . Er, sorry, I just, um . . . had a bad experience with a pig . . . as a child. As I was saying . . . this little fellow has a big future." FP hopped down from the desk, spreading a trail of corn muffin crumbs as he went. "Maybe one day he'll even be as big as my Molly."

"Your who?" Fisher said. His head was spinning. GG changed topics—and, apparently, personalities—so quickly, he had trouble following her train of thought.

"Molly." McGee picked up a small white fluffball from her lap, which had been concealed from Fisher's view because of the mounds of stuff piled on McGee's desk.

Molly turned out to be a Maltese dog, smaller than FP, covered in long, white fur. She let out an annoyed yip as

Costume Designs
for superhero FP
(per GG's suggestion)

SIR FLAPSIS BACON

THE PINK AVENGER

Option #1

Option #2

McGee lifted her up. McGee set Molly down on the floor and picked up a huge binder, handing it to Fisher. "She's my pride and joy. Just look at some of the modeling work she's done."

Fisher thumbed through the photo album halfheartedly, all the while wondering how he could turn the conversation to Two. There was Molly as a Roman senator, dressed in full togas and robes, Molly as an Elizabethan duchess, with big, fluffy sleeves and a wide ruff collar, Molly as Cinderella in a draping white thing that was apparently supposed to be a ball gown, Molly as an astronaut with a tiny space suit and a bubble helmet. . . .

"She's, um, very . . . versatile," Fisher remarked, handing the binder back to GG.

"I'm in discussions now to get her first major motion picture deal. Aren't I, Mollykins? Aren't you the most talented little . . . *Molly!*"

GG jumped up out of her chair. FP had wandered over to one side of the office, and Molly, upon seeing him, had leapt at him and begun to hump his leg enthusiastically.

"You are a *lady.*" McGee pulled Molly off the terrified-looking FP. "Sorry about that, Basley. Molly can be a little . . . rambunctious. Quite the little vixen! Like owner, like pet." McGee laughed loudly. "I'll keep her with me until we're done with our business. Speaking of which, I have just a few preliminary legal documents for you to sign. That is, unless you think you can get a better deal with Lulu O'Lunney." She chuckled a little to herself.

"Oh . . . uh, no, not at all," Fisher said. "I thought Lulu was big-time when I first met her, but . . . *clearly* you're the high-caliber one around here." He smiled so wide, he felt like his jaws would split open.

GG beamed. "Well," McGee said, "I'm glad you've come to such a reasonable conclusion."

She returned to her desk, placing Molly firmly in her lap, and reached into a drawer.

A towering stack of paper landed in front of Fisher with a *boom*.

McGee uncapped a pen and passed it over to Fisher. "Go ahead and give it your autograph."

Fisher leafed through the pages, which were filled with terms like *periodical, fiduciary, notwithstanding,* and *heretofore*. He couldn't make the slightest sense out of any of it. He wished he had Amanda with him now. His palms were sweating, and he was no closer to finding Two than when he had set foot in the office. He needed to buy some time.

"Before I sign anything," he said, "I . . . uh . . . I have to consult with my legal representative."

"Legal representative?" McGee said. "Who might that be?"

"Yours truly," said a husky female voice from behind Fisher.

He turned around and barely managed to keep his jaw in place. Amanda walked into the room wearing five-inch platform heels and a gray suit that fit her like a football jersey on a ballerina. In place of her normal glasses was a pair of mirrored aviator shades that hid half of her face.

"And you are?" GG McGee asked, wrinkling her nose and giving Amanda a once-over.

"J. Nadine Weathersby, Esquire," Amanda said, her voice rumbling as low as she could push it. "Mr. Basley's personal attorney. If you don't mind, we'll take a look at these later on." She scooped the pile of legal documents into a large briefcase. "Now, if you could arrange a cab for Mr. Basley, he must be getting back to . . . Sunset Boulevard isn't it, Basley?"

Fisher just gaped at her mutely.

"Sunset?" McGee said. "I thought you were staying on Melrose Place."

"Melrose, of course!" Amanda said. "I have so many clients, I sometimes lose track." She lowered her glasses slightly and winked subtly at Fisher. "Now come on, Mr. Basley, we have a lot of work to do." She hoisted Fisher out of his chair, swept up FP with her free arm, and handed him to Fisher. "Good day to you, Ms. McGee."

"To you, too, Ms. Weathersby," McGee said, looking

somewhat flustered. Fisher and Amanda hurried out of the office. Fisher was bursting with so many questions, he could feel them pressing at his throat. But he knew they had to wait until they were outside.

A sense of triumph was spreading, like warmth, through his chest. They had started out with an entire city to search, and had narrowed it down to a street. They were closing in on Two.

CHAPTER 10

"You saved us! How ever can we repay you? . . .
Would you like some corn?"

    —Spec script for *Out of the Flying Pan*

"This thing is heavier than a bowling ball," Amanda said, hefting the briefcase full of contract paperwork. "What was she asking you to do, sign away your soul?"

"I'm sure there's a section called 'Soul Rights and Percentages' somewhere in there," Fisher said as they walked down the sidewalk toward the bus stop. "Where did you *get* all of that stuff, anyway?" He gestured to her getup.

"Found it," Amanda said, looking straight ahead, the immense aviators sliding up and down her nose with every wobbly step. She was obviously not used to walking in heels.

"You just found it," Fisher said disbelievingly, crouching down to work FP's disguise back into place. The pig, thankfully, was sleepy after his meal in GG's office and didn't put up too much of a fight.

"Yep."

Fisher hoisted FP in his arms and fell into step again

next to Amanda. FP settled into the blanket, curling up in Fisher's arms, while the evil-looking headgear pinned his ears back and obscured most of his face.

"Well, thanks for covering me. So. We know Two lives somewhere on Melrose. What now?"

"Two is starting to attract attention," Amanda said. "I say we hit the street from one side of LA to the other. With any luck, we'll be led straight to him by a crowd of goggling fans."

Fisher noticed that Amanda choked slightly on the words "goggling fans," but he decided not to comment on it. The idea made him want to choke, too. Besides, he thought it more likely that wherever Two was staying, they would find a bunch of spicy sauce–fueled rockets shooting off the roof. His clone obviously did not know the meaning of the words *low profile*.

FP began to snore and then to shiver. He urgently shook his left foreleg, and Fisher suspected that the canine master-of-disguise, Molly, was already giving him nightmares.

As McGee's granite slab of a building fell away behind them, Fisher and Amanda passed a huge glass-walled building constructed in a giant pyramid shape. Fisher felt a cold shudder work its way down his spine. He couldn't help but think of the TechX Enterprises building; it, too, had been built like a towering pyramid. He had very nearly died in the cold, concrete depths of TechX, and he still had nightmares about racing down endless steel corridors being pursued by bizarre and twisted robot creations.

Just then, a freckly teenager bumped into him, shaking him from his reverie. The Styrofoam coffee cups the teen had been carrying toppled to the ground, splashing coffee all over the pavement.

"Hey," the kid said, brushing his moppish red hair out of his eyes. "Watch where you're—whoa." He turned back to face the doors of the pyramid building. "Hey, did you hire a stunt double or something?" he shouted.

Fisher turned to follow the redhead's gaze. For a second, he froze. Amanda froze next to him.

Walking out of the building, strutting like an astronaut who'd just gotten back from Mars in time to front a rock band, was Two. He was wearing a white button-down shirt with the sleeves rolled up to the elbows and a well-fitted pair of black, boot-cut jeans. Like everyone else's in this city, his eyes were hidden behind a pair of slick, black sunglasses.

When he saw Fisher, he lowered the shades and smiled broadly.

"Brother!" he called cheerily, striding over to where Fisher and Amanda were standing. He clapped the redhead on the shoulder. "Alex, this is my twin, Fisher.

Fisher, this is my personal assistant and protégé, Alex Barnaby."

"Oh, hello," Alex said, shaking Fisher's hand before bending down and trying to recover the coffee cups.

"Two," Fisher croaked. Adrenaline was building like liquid fire in his veins. He thought he'd have to turn Los Angeles inside out to find his clone, and within two days he'd literally walked into him. This was his chance to sort everything out. To save himself, and his clone, from an unknown and probably awful fate. He turned around to seek support from Amanda, only to find that she had vanished once again. Where had she gone this time?

"The artist formerly known as Two," Two said with an exaggerated wink. Then he turned to Alex. "You can head on home now. I'll give you a call later, okay?" Alex nodded and hurried off, cradling the cups in his arms.

Fisher felt a twinge of anxiety. Two looked like he had become comfortable with the Hollywood lifestyle. Convincing him to come back to Palo Alto without revealing the truth to him might be a pretty tough sell. And he had no idea what Two would do if he did reveal the truth.

"Where'd you get the kid?" Two asked, jerking his head at the bundle cradled in Fisher's left arm.

"This is FP," Fisher said. "I had to disguise him."

At the mention of his name, FP began to stir, and his snout poked out of the sheet. It started to twitch back and forth as FP detected the smells of two Fishers. "You have no idea how relieved I am to see you," Fisher continued. "We've been looking all over for you!"

"We?" Two said, cocking his head to the side. Fisher noticed that Two's hair seemed to be gelled into place.

"H-hey," Amanda said, stepping out from behind a parked car in her normal clothes. Fisher saw a corner of gray suit fabric sticking out of the briefcase. She smiled, looking suddenly nervous.

"Amanda!" Two cried. Then, as though realizing for the first time that he and Fisher were both standing in plain view, a look of shock crossed his face. "Amanda!" he repeated. "What are you—? How did you?" He turned to Fisher accusatorily. "You told her?!" He narrowed his eyes suspiciously and eyed Fisher up and down. "What about the big plot you told me about? The one centered in Palo Alto, and the reason that I always went to school while *you* only stayed at home and worked surveillance?"

Fisher knew he should never have lied to Two. He would have to tell Two the truth—but now was definitely not the time. Fisher pulled his clone aside, motioning for Amanda to let them have a moment.

"It's all right," Fisher whispered to Two as they turned away. "She's on our side. She's been trying to fight against our enemies for years."

Two still looked unconvinced. Fisher couldn't tell if

Two was nervous because he wasn't sure he could trust Amanda, or whether seeing her was having an entirely different effect on him. If Two really liked Amanda, as he'd seemed to before the TechX incident, maybe Fisher could use his crush to lure him home.

"We were just talking to GG McGee," Fisher said. "Trying to find out where you might be."

"Ugh," said Two, wrinkling his nose. "GG's a nosy, talkative iguana. Lulu O'Lunney really knows what she's doing."

"Is that who you were seeing in there?" Fisher asked, glancing back at the huge building. FP was wriggling around in his arms, his nose still sniffing in Two's direction. Fisher squeezed his arms around FP to try and keep him from escaping.

"That's right," Two said. "She got me an audition for

the Spot-Rite gig. Can you believe it? One step closer to finding our mother. This stuff tastes terrible, by the way," he added, holding up a bottle of the new, edible Spot-Rite. "It's like somebody ground up an old tire and made iced tea with it. By the way—I'm going by Basley around here." He grinned at Amanda, who gave a small, uncertain-looking smile back. She kept adjusting the briefcase in her grip, moving it around and switching it from hand to hand.

"Basley Bas," Fisher said drily.

"That's right," Two said, flashing a film-star smile. "Girls really love it," he said in a slightly louder voice, as though to be sure Amanda could hear him. Fisher saw Amanda's smile flatten. FP was struggling harder in Fisher's arms.

"How did you survive that blast at TechX?" Fisher said. "I was a hundred yards away and it still knocked me flat."

Two's face grew serious. "Dr. X and I were fighting," Two said. "Everything was falling down around us, and I knew the building was about to blow. Then I saw a couple of the robot prototypes coming up the corridor. They had rocket propulsion built into their frames. I made a bolt for one. Dr. X grabbed at me as I jumped, and pulled out a clump of my hair." He tilted his head to the side and pointed to a spot behind his left ear where a little tuft was slowly growing back. "But I was able to leap onto the robot and, by blind luck, I triggered its rockets and sped out through a collapsed part of the roof into the sky. I landed hundreds of miles away—luckily, the rocket dropped me directly into Lake Powell. As it happened, I wasn't too far from here."

"That's . . . that's impossible," Fisher said, shaking his head.

"Improbable," Two said. "In fact, the likelihood of my survival was exactly one in 1,072,001." Two raised his eyebrows at Amanda.

Amanda crossed her arms quickly across her chest and gave him a thin, terse smile. "Wow. Pretty amazing," she said flatly.

Two frowned. "It *was* amazing—and dangerous. And moving to LA wasn't much better at first. This city is huge! It will eat you up and spit you out."

"Oh, we know," Amanda said, maintaining the steel in her eyes. "We've been through a lot of it trying to find you."

FP was snapping his tiny jaws together inches from Two's arm.

"In any event," Fisher jumped in quickly, wrapping the blanket over FP's head, "it's great that we bumped into you. Now we can help you get home!"

"Home?" Two said. "That place isn't my home. Our

mother is *here*. When I realized I was in LA, something clicked in my memory. I remembered seeing Mom in the Spot-Rite commercials. She must be close by. After all this time, we can finally be reunited with her. Isn't that incredible?"

Fisher wished, more than anything, that he had never told Two that a commercial actress was his real mother. He had done it in a moment of desperation, when Two first emerged from his test tube. But he couldn't tell the truth now; he just couldn't. Two would never come home, and he'd never trust Fisher again.

"Besides," Two went on, "life is so much better here! My agent set me up with an apartment. I don't even have to pay rent. I'm going to lots of auditions, meeting important people, going to parties, dinners, dinner parties . . ."

"I see," Amanda said, hugging herself. "That's what's keeping you here. The glamorous lifestyle."

"No," Two said, turning to her with a sigh of exasperation. "I have a job to get done. The quality of living around here is just a bonus."

Amanda looked away. "There are . . . there are things in Palo Alto worth coming back to," she said softly. Then she cleared her throat.

"Name one," Two said. Amanda whipped around, and Fisher saw a black flame flare up in her eyes. He hastily stepped between them.

"Listen," Fisher said, jostling Two a little to get his attention. "We're in danger. We . . ." He glanced at the glowering Amanda, silently pleading with her not to judge him for the lies he was about to tell. "The guards know something strange is going on and they contacted their allies. Agents have been following me. They might have found you. And they *might* even know that our mother's here. Look. . . ." Fisher pulled the threatening note out of his pocket and handed it to Two, who studied it for a minute, turning it over in his hand.

"Well then," said Two, with a deep breath, "we need to speed up the effort to find our mother."

"What?!" Fisher said. "We can't risk that! We have to lie low, wait for this to blow over."

"I appreciate your caution," Two said. "I know you're just trying to protect Mom." Fisher could feel Amanda's angry glare on him, burning the back of his neck like a laser. "But sooner or later we have to take action. We can't keep a lid on this forever, you know."

Fisher had no response to that. He turned to Amanda, who was now refusing to look at either of them, and was instead pretending to be interested in a nearby wastepaper basket. Her expression very clearly read: "I am done speaking with both of you."

"It's been great seeing you . . . both of you," Two said breezily, although Fisher thought his smile looked a little forced, and he kept glancing over at Amanda. "But I'm afraid that's my ride." He pointed to a sleek black town car pulling up to the curb. "I have an audition in half an hour, and this evening I'm going to make an appearance at a costume party at the Hollywood Bowl. Don't worry, I'll be in touch soon."

"What?" Amanda said, finally turning to him with a sour expression. "No Rolls-Royce? No personal helicopter?"

"I'll let you know when I get one of those," Two shot back. "You look like you could stand to be in low air pressure for a while."

Before Amanda could react, he stepped into the opening door of the car and was whisked away into the sunlit streets.

Two's words echoed in Fisher's head as the car pulled away. *We can't keep a lid on this forever, you know.*

≋ CHAPTER 11 ≋

When the floor's fallen out from under you enough times,
you start to think, maybe the problem isn't a weak floor.
Maybe it's that you've got saw blades for shoes.

—Fisher Bas, Personal Notes

As Fisher watched the car roll away, he deeply regretted
not packing his magnetic harpoon gun. Granted, the last
time he'd tried to use it he'd ended up being slung right
into the waffle-cone storage at the back of an ice-cream
truck, but even a desperate tactic seemed better than
nothing at this point. Two didn't want to come home—
and even worse, Fisher couldn't blame him.

Two was living a dream life in LA. Free housing,
no parents, no school, rising fame, a whole city to play
around in . . .

In comparison, Wompalog Middle School seemed about
as exciting as a chess tournament in a nursing home.
And Wompalog was the only other place Two had ever
known, thanks to Fisher. Fisher had thrown Two into
that festering pit of horror so that he wouldn't have to
suffer through it himself.

Blueprints for
MAGNETIC
HARPOON GUN

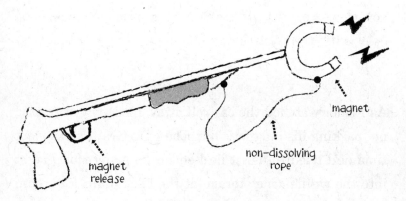

It was hard to blame Two for wanting to escape. It was what Fisher had wanted, too.

But Two had to come home. The stakes had gotten too high. Fisher knew he was being followed—the note proved it. Agents could be trailing Two right now. This time next week, Fisher could be in a cell on the far side of the moon, and Two could be in a laboratory.

Fisher felt his stomach dip into the soles of his shoes.

"Just what *exactly* was all that talk about sinister agents and evil conspiracies?" Amanda demanded as they watched the car disappear into the blur of traffic.

"I told you I had to lie to him to keep him in line," Fisher protested. He didn't like the way Amanda was looking at him.

"I guess I didn't expect you to just keep on doing it," she said, little embers still smoldering in her eyes. "You got me to agree to help you by telling me the truth. How do you expect to ever earn his trust if you don't do the same for him?"

"I will!" Fisher cried out. He passed a hand through his hair. "Just not now."

"Right." Amanda shook her head almost pityingly.

"So what now?" Fisher said, despondent.

Amanda exhaled. "I have a plan."

"Can't wait to hear it," Fisher said hollowly.

"We know he'll be at the Hollywood Bowl tonight," she said. "That place is huge. I'm sure sneaking in won't be too hard."

"And what do you plan to say to him? And that's *if* we find him." Fisher said. "Like you said, the place is huge."

Fisher leaned down and freed FP from his disguise so that he could trot around for a little while. The little pig started snuffling around at his feet.

"I'm going to try the guilt angle. I plan on telling him," Amanda said, coughing a bit and aiming her eyes directly at the sidewalk, "that I have a huge crush on him, and that if he doesn't come back to Palo Alto with us my heart will split down the middle and never recover."

"So you yell at me because I didn't tell him the truth, but you're going to lie about having feelings for him?" Fisher asked cautiously. She hadn't exactly looked pleased to see him earlier, despite Two's obvious attempts at impressing her.

"Do you want him back or don't you?" Amanda snapped. "My methods have been getting us along pretty well so far. Don't start doubting them now. Besides, who are you to judge me for lying to him?"

Fisher held up his hands in a gesture of surrender. "I'm not questioning your methods," Fisher said quickly. He paused, considering. "And your idea isn't bad. I had a conversation with Two about you a few weeks ago, and I think he might genuinely like you."

"Wait—what? Really?" Amanda squeaked. Then she coughed and grunted, and resumed in a normal voice: "Well . . . good then. If that's the case, then there's an even better chance my plan will work. Come on."

Fisher scooped up FP, who was having a staring contest with a seagull over a discarded half sandwich, and he and Amanda began the long trek back to the King of Hollywood.

The Southern California sun felt a lot less pleasant after Fisher had spent half an hour marching under it at a pace that would give a drill sergeant an asthma attack. The taxi to GG McGee's office had used up what little cash he and Amanda had been given by their parents, so they'd had to walk back. Amanda's legs were short, but they powered forward like she had a diesel engine embedded in her hip bones. Fisher could barely feel his own legs, and FP's weight was tugging on his arms like a lead brick. Sweat was dripping from his eyelids by the time they finally made it.

"Fisher Bas," Mr. Dubel, one of the chaperones, had just called as Fisher and Amanda slipped through the door of the hotel and joined the rest of their classmates.

"H-heeeere," Fisher managed to gasp out, worming his way into the line.

Mr. Dubel's dim eyes noted Fisher's presence, and he moved on in the roll call.

Ms. Snapper stood in front of the group, her arms crossed, trying to suppress a bitter frown.

"She doesn't look too happy," Fisher said to Amanda, pointing to their teacher. "I wonder how long she stood around waiting for Dr. Devilish to show."

"Long enough that our absence went totally unnoticed," Amanda replied. "That's all I care about."

Fisher thought, not for the first time, that he must be very careful to stay on Amanda's good side.

Once the class had been tallied up in the hotel lobby, the group headed out to the bus. Fisher didn't enjoy having to walk again after barely catching his breath, but at least it was to a bus with comfortable seats.

The *Strange Science* set was a very different place in the middle of a shoot. All of the crew members sat or stood quietly at their assigned stations, monitoring screens or sound apparatus. The lighting was on full force, illuminating Dr. Devilish and his laboratory in a yellow-tinged blaze. The class sat on cushioned seats set on risers behind the cameras. FP sat happily at Fisher's side, free of his disguise. FP seemed to enjoy being free of the frightening steel headgear so much that he was willing to sit still for a while.

Lucy Fir looked out of sorts as she walked onto the set wearing athletic pants and a Lakers T-shirt.

"Can you page someone from wardrobe for me, please?" she snapped at a nearby stagehand. "I'm missing my best suit. I want to know if it got mixed in with their things."

Fisher looked over at Amanda and raised an eyebrow. She shrugged, but he saw the smile flicker across her face. No wonder her disguise had been so ill-fitting. Lucy was nearly a foot taller than Amanda.

"Welcome to *Strange Science*," Dr. Devilish said as the bright film lights turned his full smile into its own constellation. "Today's episode: "Fur Spots and Kilowatts." And now," Dr. Devilish said, locking his eyes on the middle of three cameras and treating the audience to his famously dazzling smile, "for our first experiment of the day, I will demonstrate how to power a lightbulb using the most unusual-seeming combination of ingredients: a handful of dried apricots—and a wombat."

Fisher leaned forward eagerly, straining to get a better view.

Dr. Devilish gestured to a large lightbulb on his lab table. It was fitted with a metal frame and run through with a prong, so that an electrical current could be passed through it.

He then reached into a drawer and set a small bag of apricots on the table. Finally, he ducked behind the table and came up with a small gray mammal with a round face in his hands. "Behold; Wally!" he said. A chorus of very quiet "aww"s arose from the audience.

The sleepy-looking wombat plodded in a small circle around the table, its eyes unfocused and vaguely confused, as though dazzled by all the lights. Dr. Devilish removed two crinkly, dried apricots from the bag, and carefully placed one on the end of each of the mechanism's prongs.

"By harnessing the natural conductivity of the apricot and the electrochemical properties inherent to wombats," he said, giving the camera a dashing toss of his head on the word *wombats*, "I can create an electric current strong enough to power this bulb for several minutes."

"Is that really possible, Fisher?" Veronica whispered in

his ear as she sat down next to him. He seized up slightly at the feeling of her breath and turned to answer.

"Well, I . . . Well, it could . . . I've never really studied wombats, but maybe. . . ." Veronica turned back to watch Dr. Devilish, and Fisher found his attention badly torn between the two of them.

Dr. Devilish pulled out several more apricots and stuck them to the first two with quick-drying adhesive. As a final step, he gently held the wombat's front paw up until it clasped one side of the apricot circuit, and lifted its tail to touch the other. Fisher winced as the bulb winked on quite brightly. The audience gasped, and Fisher found himself clapping along with everyone else. . . . Everyone except Ms. Snapper, who was scowling.

"And now," Dr. Devilish said. "You can see that the—"

He was drowned out by a loud crackling sound. The lightbulb went out and so did several of the studio lights. One of the cameramen stepped back from his camera with a frown and checked its power cord.

"What happened?" Lucy Fir rushed forward as various crew members began shouting instructions to one another.

"Problem in a power cable," said one of the crew. He lifted up a large cable, following it hand over hand, searching for the problem. He'd pulled several feet onto the stage when the problem became clear: FP was pulled into view, his jaws locked around the cable with fierce determination.

Fisher leapt out of his seat and bounded down the risers. He'd been so focused on Dr. Devilish—and Veronica—that he hadn't even noticed FP had left his side. He unhooked his pig's mandibles from the cable.

"I'm sorry, I'm so sorry," he said, his face burning hot as the lights had a minute earlier. He kneeled down and whispered to FP. "One more embarrassment, and you'll be wearing Trevor's headgear for the rest of your life."

As he turned to apologize to Dr. Devilish, he noticed a thin electric cable, only visible from this vantage point, snaking from the bulb apparatus on top of the lab table to the larger cable FP had been chewing.

A cold feeling flooded Fisher.

"Wait a second," he said. "The lightbulbs were *plugged in*?"

"Uh." A slight flush crept over Dr. Devilish's tan cheeks. "Yes, naturally." He coughed and adjusted his collar. "You see, sometimes the wombat will generate *such* power that the assembly won't be able to handle the circuit, so we run a cable to reroute any excess electricity." His toothy smile popped back onto his face, and he hurriedly disassembled the setup. "Let's move on to the next segment," he announced loudly, clapping his hands. He was so eager to move on, he neglected to put Wally back in his cage.

Fisher was trying to gather FP up into his arms when

Wally the Wombat ran up to them. He started sniffing and lightly pawing Fisher all over, then did the same with FP, who tried to swat the little animal away with his front hoof.

"C'mere, Wally!" said Henry, the sound engineer Fisher had met earlier, running up to them and tapping his hands on the ground. "Come on, boy! Leave them alone, now." Wally gave Fisher and FP one last, wide-eyed look before scampering into Henry's arms.

"Wow. He responds to your commands?" Fisher said as Henry scooped the wombat up.

"Sometimes," Henry said. "Ever since he arrived on set I've been trying to train him. I'm thinking there may be a future in domesticated wombats as pets! I might even start my own business if I get tired of doing sound."

"That, uh, sounds great," Fisher said. "I'm sure you'll corner the market on wombats. . . . I think I should get back to my seat."

"Right!" Henry said. "See you later! Come on, Wally."

The next experiment continued with the small mammals theme. Dr. Devilish constructed a water filtration system using only a few handfuls of oak leaves (as the filter itself) and a very indignant lemur (whose footpads apparently contained antimicrobial chemicals that, when stomped repeatedly on a pile of leaves, gave them germ-killing properties).

This time the experiment and filming went without a hitch. Fisher eyed the little water samples that got passed out to the class with suspicion, but they looked clean. Maybe Dr. Devilish *did* know what he was doing. The taping wrapped up smoothly, and the class was gathering up to leave. Fisher kept a tight hold on FP.

"Fisher, could I talk to you for a moment?" Veronica said, walking up to him. Fisher mentally scanned through all of the different ways he knew to say yes.

"B-but of course," he got out at last, and then cursed himself for sounding like a French waiter.

Veronica pulled him away from the class.

"I just wanted to say that I really liked your new video," she said.

"My . . . new video," Fisher said, feeling like he had just swallowed a squirming wombat.

"Yeah, it was very clever," Veronica said, smiling. "It looks like you're really attracting a fan base. I guess there's still a lot I don't know about you, Fisher."

"Well . . ." Fisher choked out, past the flailing sensation in his stomach. "It's . . . difficult, managing two different lives. I'd like to be more honest about everything I do, but I know I can't right now." He was relieved to finally tell her something that wasn't technically a lie.

"I understand," she said, tossing her shimmering hair over one shoulder. "Look . . . this might sound kind of weird, but do you think I could ask a favor?"

"Of course!" Fisher blurted instinctively. "Anything."

"Do you think maybe . . . you could introduce me to Kevin Keels?"

Fisher's brief moment of happiness was overwhelmed like a candle being hit by a tsunami.

"I don't really know him that well. . . ." he began. But then, seeing Veronica's smile falter, he quickly mumbled, "But I'll see what I can do."

"Thanks so much, Fisher!" she said, leaning in and giving him a warm hug. Under any other circumstance, this gesture would have sent Fisher spiraling onto cloud nine. But she might as well have been wearing a jellyfish-tentacle sweater.

The wombat in Fisher's stomach had turned into a bowling ball. How could someone like Veronica like someone like Kevin so much? Unless . . . unless he was mistaken about Veronica. Maybe she wasn't really as dazzling and incredible as he thought she was.

And why on earth had he said he would try to introduce them?

And what had Veronica meant about his "new video"?

Things were spiraling out of control. Two's notoriety was growing by the hour.

A thought hit him like an icicle between the eyes: if Two was so much better known, so beloved and so multitalented . . . and he still had all of Fisher's smarts and ingenuity . . . what purpose did Fisher serve?

What claim did he have to being the definitive Fisher? Why shouldn't *he* be Fisher-2? Did he have anything that made him stand out, that made him unique or even interesting, when compared to his increasingly more popular clone?

≫ CHAPTER 12 ≪

*When executing a bold mission, you have to be careful that
you don't get too excited and leap into the trap you've laid
for your enemy. . . . Unless, of course, you're a specifically
designed trap-leaping robot.*

—Vic Daring (Issue #78)

Fisher had never thought it possible, but he was actually
starting to get tired of the constant diet of star-shaped
fries and special sauce. He found himself actually missing
his mom's Massive Zucchini Blast Salad.

"How are we going to slip away tonight, then?" Amanda
whispered to Fisher as the class was lining up to head
into the restaurant. "She won't fall for the same trick
twice. Did you see how she was glaring at Dr. Devilish
all day?"

"I think I have an idea," Fisher said. "Play along." With
that, he unwrapped FP from his blanket. He then put on
a pair of lab gloves—he always had a pair handy—and
grabbed a special cloth from his pocket. It contained a
substance that reacted with the pigment in the top layer
of skin and could alter it instantly. On Fisher, the invention made the uneven red patches on his skin—a result

of frequent humiliated blushing and the sun's harshness to his skin—even out, but he correctly guessed it would have a different effect on FP's skin chemistry.

Fisher rubbed FP from head to tail, and the pig started to change from uniform pink to a blotchy green.

"Follow my lead," he muttered to her as he walked up to Ms. Snapper. Amanda followed behind, staring at FP's transformation.

"Ms. . . . Ms. Snapper?" Fisher said.

"Yes, Fisher?" Ms. Snapper replied.

"I'm afraid FP has had an allergic reaction," he said with a pitying look in his eyes. "Amanda fed him something from her lunch that he wasn't supposed to eat." Ms. Snapper's eyes widened as FP turned greener on the spot. "It's not serious, but I need to give him some medicine and keep an eye on him for a while." Fisher nudged Amanda's foot with his toe.

"I feel really bad about it," Amanda said, stepping right into stride with Fisher's con. "If it's okay, I'd like to go along with Fisher and help him take care of the poor little guy."

"Oh dear . . . well, all right," Ms. Snapper said. "He certainly looks like he could use your attention. If you want, you can go and help Fisher with him."

Fisher and Amanda sped up to the seventh floor, then split up and headed for their respective rooms.

Once inside his hotel room, Fisher made straight for his suitcase, reaching underneath his everyday clothing and removing his Spy Suit. The sleek, black, full-body suit had seen him through his mission to rescue Two from TechX. Its pockets and pouches were outfitted with specialized tools and gadgets Fisher had invented. It would work well as a costume and might come in handy if they got into any trouble. And when it came to Two, trouble was one thing Fisher could count on.

Besides, after the suit had seen him safely through the disaster at TechX, Fisher imagined that maybe the suit was a kind of good-luck charm—and it was obvious he needed one now more than ever.

"Okay, boy," Fisher said to FP, who was curled in front of the air conditioner as the pigment change began to wear off. "I'm going to be back in a little while, okay? Try not to mess with any of my stuff. Or any of Warren's," he said, pointing to the large suitcase sitting next to the room's other bed.

He cracked his door open very slowly and peeked out into the hallway. It was empty. A moment later, he saw Amanda's door inch open. They stayed in place for a few seconds, checking that the hallway remained clear.

Fisher took a deep breath and slipped out of his room. Amanda followed suit. She was wearing her wrestling unitard, in Wompalog's navy blue and pumpkin-orange school colors. Fisher subtly raised an eyebrow, but Amanda's icy expression kept his mouth shut. They met at the stairwell.

"Ready?" she asked, cracking her knuckles.

"Ready," Fisher answered, adjusting the fit of his suit. It felt a little tighter than it had last time he'd worn it. Maybe all the spicy fries were having their inevitable consequences.

The stairs were empty, and they made it to the ground floor with ease. They slipped through a side door that led on to the parking lot.

"All right, I've gotten us away from Ms. Snapper," Fisher said. "How are we going to get to the Hollywood Bowl?"

"Follow me," Amanda said.

They ducked low and tried to conceal themselves behind a line of shrubs as they made their way past the hotel. Cars whizzed in and out of the parking lot, and people filed past, but nobody took a second look at Fisher and Amanda, even with their unusual attire.

Through a large gap in the shrubbery, Fisher got a sudden unobstructed view of the restaurant's windows. Ms. Snapper was scanning the parking lot—looking almost exactly in their direction.

"Amanda!" he whispered frantically. Just as the teacher's gaze was about to reach them, a taxi pulled up to the curb, and Fisher wrenched Amanda behind it. They crouched down and watched as the passengers filed out the other side.

Fisher was breathing so hard, he couldn't speak for a moment. The engine vibrated against his back.

Two young men walked up to the driver.

"Hey, man," one of them said. "Do you think you could give us a lift to the Hollywood Bowl?"

Fisher couldn't believe his luck. He felt a surge of adrenaline. Amanda looked at him, eyes wide, and then gestured to the trunk.

"Can you—?" Amanda began.

"I can," Fisher said, reaching into one of his Spy Suit's back pouches and pulling a small canister out. It was his latest spy item, Key in a Can, and this would be its first field test. He pressed the nozzle and sprayed a fine mist into the trunk keyhole. Instantly, the substance began to solidify, filling up the lock in the exact shape of its key. In moments, a gray plastic key-like object had formed, and Fisher turned it. The trunk popped open instantly, and Fisher and Amanda slipped in.

It was stuffy and hot and smelled like a dozen hockey pucks in a toaster oven. Amanda followed him in, curling up against one side so that she would be mostly concealed from view if the trunk opened again. Fisher sighed and pushed himself up against the other side, feeling the

Designs for
KEY IN A CAN

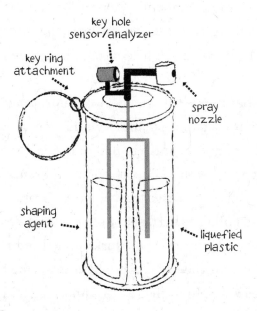

key hole
sensor/analyzer

key ring
attachment

spray
nozzle

shaping
agent

liquefied
plastic

sweat begin to roll down his neck and arms. He reached up and eased the trunk closed. It was nearly pitch-black now, and the heat became even more stifling. Then the engine gunned, filling their ears with a washed-out roar, and Fisher lurched as the taxi pulled away from the curb.

Fisher bounced up and down as the cab picked up speed, until he felt like a popcorn kernel just ready to pop. Each time he hit his head against the trunk, he felt another burst of worry. He still had no idea what he was going to do even if they succeeded in bringing Two back to Palo Alto. Would they keep on switching places, pretending to be the same person for the rest of their lives? Would Two take on another persona, somehow disguise himself and create a new life as someone else entirely?

Or, Fisher wondered, would Two simply take his place? With Two's newfound popularity and ever-growing confidence, he might be daring enough to really do it.

Fisher was feeling like a popcorn kernel about to *explode* by the time the taxi came to a stop. Working quickly, he pulled a small set of pliers out of a side pocket of his Spy Suit and went to work unlatching the trunk. Amanda caught the door as it began to spring open, and they rolled out behind the car, Amanda softly closing the trunk behind them.

The sun was setting, but it was still light enough outside to blind Fisher for a few seconds. He shook his head, trying to clear the dizziness from his vision.

The Hollywood Bowl was a huge outdoor amphitheater. Tiers of seats, carved out of the side of a hill, sloped downward to a small stage area. Thankfully, there were so many people crowding around them that nobody seemed to have noticed the fact that they had arrived via the trunk of a taxi.

A huge banner stretched above them: it read CLOAKED JUSTICE—WRAP PARTY. Fisher had heard of the superhero TV show, though he'd never seen it. Everyone streaming into the party was wearing a costume, most of them superhero spandex, which meant that he and Amanda actually blended in well.

The big stage at the bottom of the bowl seemed to be the center of the party: waiters circulated with trays of food, a DJ was playing dance music, and bartenders were serving up drinks. Other people milled around among the seats. There must have been a thousand guests.

Fisher sucked in a deep breath. "He's going to be at the center of everything," he said, pointing to the stage. "He's allergic to staying low profile."

"Lead the way," Amanda said. For once, she sounded nervous.

Fisher and Amanda reached the upper tier of seats and saw their first obstacle: a security barrier set up in front of them. There were four entrance points, each guarded by three massive bodyguards. The arriving guests either had badges to prove that they worked on the show, carried special guest tickets, or were famous enough that the guards recognized them on sight.

"What now?" Amanda asked.

"I'm thinking." Fisher frowned, scanning the crowd.

"There." He pointed to a man dressed as one of the talking trees from *The Wizard of Oz*. It was a huge, elaborate costume with branches and leaves sticking out on all sides. He had to walk very slowly to make sure he didn't swipe anyone with a dangling limb.

"Tree-man?" Amanda wrinkled her nose. "What about him?"

Fisher slipped off the narrow pack on his back. "This is a prototype for my new model Shrub-in-a-Backpack. It's a camouflage device. My last one was confiscated."

"How?" Amanda said.

"I took it into TechX. It went off by accident, and I was captured."

"Correct me if I'm wrong, but isn't getting captured the *opposite* of the point of camouflage?"

"Well, I was dangling off a balcony at the time. . . ." Fisher said, then shook his head. "Anyway, this one doesn't deploy yet, but we can still use it." Fisher opened the bag up and pulled out two metal-and-plastic bundles, which he rapidly unfolded into close imitations of thick, leafy branches. "Okay, you take one and I'll take one. We're going to get as close to the tree-man as possible. Follow his movements. If we hurry we can sneak up behind him just before he walks past security."

Amanda looked at the branch, then at the man in the tree suit, then at the security.

"Okay, let's go," she said with a sigh. Fisher could tell she wished she had a better idea.

The tree-man trundled forward, branches swaying back and forth. Fisher and Amanda crept up behind him and eased their branches into place. The large, leafy branch concealed Fisher entirely. He couldn't see Amanda—or anything else, for that matter. All he could do was shuffle forward a little at a time, praying he and Amanda would remain invisible.

Every time the tree-man paused, Fisher's breath stopped with him, terrified that someone had spotted him. Fisher tried to comfort himself with the idea that people had been concealing themselves behind trees for thousands of years. On the other hand, most trees didn't walk or have to pass through security at a swanky Hollywood party.

Fisher recalled a recent Vic Daring comic, in which Vic had to hide himself among a forest of plants with venomous spines and a taste for the human spleen. So it could be worse.

It felt like a day had passed when the man finally got through security and pushed into the crowd flowing down toward the stage. Fisher broke away from the tree-man, re-collapsing his branch. Amanda handed him the other one.

"Good work." She flashed him a rare smile, and Fisher was surprised to see how pretty she looked when she wasn't scowling—or hitting him. With her smarts and looks, he was starting to understand how Two, someone that she didn't frequently threaten to clobber, might have feelings for her.

"Thanks," Fisher said. "Any sign of him?" He ducked under the felt tail of a man in an orange tyrannosaurus costume.

"Not yet," Amanda said. "It's too crowded. We should split up, find him faster. Let's meet back here in fifteen minutes."

"All right," Fisher said. "I'll go left." He squirmed between a pair of astronauts and almost tripped on a pink-and-red-silk fairy wing.

The central area was being used as the dance floor, with the DJ against the back wall. Partygoers stood around the periphery of the dance floor, holding drinks and small plates of food. Fisher was glad that FP was back at the hotel. He'd be scrambling around in a frenzy with so much food everywhere.

Fisher was pushing his way toward the stage, when out of the corner of his eye he saw two tall men in black suits and dark sunglasses, wires trailing conspicuously from their ears. Alarms screamed in Fisher's brain. He threw himself behind the robed legs of a partygoer dressed as a medieval friar. It was only when he stuck his head back around the monk's costume, and saw the two "agents" remove their sunglasses to reveal the faces of actors Fisher recognized, that his lungs remembered to breathe.

Fisher straightened up and found that his head was spinning. The aftereffects of the hot, cramped ride in the taxi trunk, the stress, and the bustling crowd made Fisher feel dizzy. He spotted a plastic thermos with something dark green in it sitting on a chair and made for it. He gulped down half of the thick liquid in a few seconds. It soothed his dry throat, but it tasted like a bag of lawn mower clippings and powdered thornbush. Soon afterward, his stomach started roiling. He didn't know what was in the weird smoothie, and unfortunately, his body didn't seem to, either.

He saw a sign pointing the way to restrooms, and stumbled toward them, muttering apologies as he ricocheted between people like a pinball on a zigzag trajectory. He walked through one of the stage doors in the wings, down a short hallway, and found the bathroom on his left. He went into a stall, kneeling in front of the toilet and breathing heavily. After a minute or two, the whirlpool in his gut started to subside. He didn't feel great, but he didn't feel like everything he'd eaten for the past day was about to rapidly retrace its steps, either.

Another few minutes passed, and he felt recovered enough to resume the search. He was about to stand up and return to the party when the bathroom door banged open.

"I can't keep doing this," a boy was saying in a qua- vering, tearful tone. "Every week it gets harder to hide the truth. Sooner or later people will find out, and I'll be laughed right out of my career."

It took Fisher a second to place the voice: it was Kevin Keels! There was no doubt about it. Fisher stayed where he was, almost afraid to breathe.

"You'll keep it up because that's what you're paid to do," snarled the unmistakable voice of GG McGee. "You were handpicked to be the next teen sensation because you look like a Greek god and can smile for hours at a time. The fact that you once turned a car radio into a fireworks display just by singing along has nothing to do with it."

Fisher's sweat dried up, leaving him cold. Kevin Keels . . . was a fraud? Was nothing in this city real?

"You keep smiling," GG McGee went on, "and mouth- ing the words to whatever popular slop you're given, and I'll keep the paychecks coming. Are we clear on that?"

"We're clear," Kevin replied in a sheepish voice. A moment later, Fisher heard the door slam again.

He quickly and quietly exited the stall. He couldn't help but wonder what Veronica would think of the famous Kevin if she knew that he was a phony, but he had to focus on finding Two. He'd wasted enough time already.

He was pushing his way back toward the stage when he spotted Amanda leaning against the wall, her face bitter and angry. Fisher made his way over to her.

"I found him," she said flatly.

"You did?" Fisher burst out. He looked around. "So where is he?"

"He's not coming," she said, her eyes flashing angrily. "He says that Hollywood is his home now. He told me that his life in Palo Alto is in the past, and he intends to keep it there."

"Oh, no . . ." Fisher swallowed hard and raked a hand through his hair. "Come on—we have to try and reason with him!"

"Forget it," Amanda said, her expression stony. "The deal is off, Fisher. You want him back, you can get him yourself."

"But—" Fisher said, but didn't get to protest anymore. Amanda pushed herself off the wall and then shoved him out of her way.

"I said *forget it*!" She stormed away through the crowd as Fisher stumbled backward, tripped over a folded-up chair and fell, arms flailing, straight into one of the buffet tables.

The thin legs of the buffet table buckled, and the end Fisher landed on collapsed. The table's other end sprang up, launching a chocolate cupcake through the air like a five-hundred-calorie badminton birdie. The cupcake splattered into the back of a young man standing at the other end of the buffet, wearing a jungle explorer costume. He turned around in surprise, to see GG McGee, who raised her arms innocently.

Smirking, the man picked a small raspberry tart off the table next to him and flicked it right into McGee's forehead. Flabbergasted, she retaliated with a cupful of lemonade to the man's face. The fight escalated: more cupcakes, then pies, then full-sized cakes, and more people started to join in. Fisher decided to take the opportunity to slip away.

As he did, he noticed two other actors wearing special agent costumes—dark suit, dark sunglasses, earpieces— a little ways off in the crowd. He started at the sight, then took a breath and reminded himself that he was safe. They were just actors, dressed in costume.

Weren't they?

He turned around—and spotted another two people dressed as spies. They were moving resolutely toward him, and neither one was carrying a drink or a plate of food. Instead, they were shoving their way through the crowd.

The pounding of his veins was painful against the tight collar of his Spy Suit. He hurled himself into the thickest part of the crowd, crashing into cowboys and knights, werewolves and androids. Some of them leapt and shouted. Others were so big they didn't even notice him.

He pushed through a forest of legs, sliding and squeezing through the narrowest spots he could find in the hope of losing his larger pursuers. A few hurried glances over his shoulder made it seem that they were falling behind.

Fisher kept barreling blindly in the direction he thought would lead him up and out of the Bowl. He pounded up the incline, as colorful costumes turned to blur around him. Finally, he crashed through the edge of the crowd and stumbled dizzily out of one of the entrances to the Hollywood Bowl. He ran, gasping, down the street, just as a bus pulled up. He frantically clambered up the two steps to the door as it opened and managed to sputter, "King . . . King of Holly . . . Hotel?" before gasping in another breath.

"Yeah, yeah, get in, kid," said the short, gray-haired bus driver, chuckling to himself.

He fumbled in one of the emergency pockets of his Spy Suit, and miraculously found he had enough change for the fare.

He wondered briefly if he should have looked for Amanda, but shook the notion away. Amanda had a head start on him, and *she* wasn't being pursued by spies. She'd proven herself very capable of just about anything. She probably could've jogged all the way back by now. Besides, Fisher had his and his clone's lives to worry about.

On the way back to the hotel, he kept his head down and pulled his legs up into his stomach. He was all alone again. Whoever was after him was closing in on him, and his plan was spiraling out of control. If he didn't find a way to grab Two and run, he'd end up somewhere in Nevada in a prison disguised as an abandoned barn. And Two could be reduced to a few thousand slides on a microscope.

What had happened between Two and Amanda that made her so upset? What could Fisher say to convince Two to come home now?

And if Two wouldn't give up his new life . . . would Fisher be forced to give up his?

CHAPTER 13

I'd rather be around strangers who are curious about me than friends who don't really care.

—Two, Personal Journal

The lights were blazing, the cameras were ready to roll, and the craft services table was still in one piece; it was a busy day on the bustling *Strange Science* set. Dr. Devilish stood very still as one of his patented "beard-bots" buzzed around him, its multiple arms whirring, neatly trimming his goatee. Little whisker bits flew into the air, forming a blurry dark cloud around him.

Amanda stood deliberately away from Fisher. He'd seen her briefly in the hallway when he'd returned the night before, but she'd gone on walking with a wallpaper-stripping scowl that made him keep his distance.

Once again, the class was watching from the risers behind the camera as assistants helped with the final setup of the lab. This episode was going to involve special guest participation, and so many of the kids excitedly chatted with one another and tried to gain the still-grooming Dr. Devilish's attention in the hopes that they might be chosen as a volunteer.

This was it. The last day in LA. With suited agents closing in all around him and a renegade clone bent on superstardom. If he didn't take decisive action today, if he didn't find a way to pull himself out of the deep, dark hole that he'd dug himself into, it would cave in all around him.

He was so preoccupied, he'd even let FP wander away from him. The pig was probably finding something new to knock over or chew through already, but he couldn't bring himself to care. There were two Fishers, but events were moving toward there being zero pretty soon.

He looked over at Amanda, who had deliberately chosen to sit as far away from Fisher as possible. He wanted to ask more about what, exactly, Two had said to her, but he wanted to plan his approach carefully. Amanda hadn't spoken to him since the Hollywood Bowl, and he didn't want to drive her off even more.

Veronica was huddled with her friends, chatting about Kevin Keels. Apparently, he was scheduled to make a guest appearance on an upcoming *Strange Science* episode. Fisher's blood began to simmer. He wished he'd thought to record the conversation he'd overheard between Kevin and GG, but he'd been so shocked, he hadn't even thought to whip out his pocket AV equipment.

Fisher scanned the room for FP and finally spotted him, trotting out from behind Dr. Devilish's worktable.

Close on his heels was Wally the Wombat, who had supposedly powered the lightbulb in the previous day's experiment. They started what looked like some kind of game. FP would look back at Wally, then stretch out his forelegs a few times, before running forward and hopping into the air. Wally would then try to copy what he did.

Was FP trying to teach Wally how to fly?

Fisher shook his head, cracking a smile for the first time in what felt like forever. At least FP was enjoying LA.

"Ms. Snapper?" said Lucy Fir, walking up to the teacher. Fisher noticed she had retrieved her suit.

"Oh, Ms. Fir," Ms. Snapper said with a flat smile. "What can I do for you?"

"On behalf of *Strange Science*, I'd like to thank you and your class for your visit and present you with this," Lucy said, handing a framed, autographed eight by ten headshot of Dr. Devilish to Ms. Snapper.

"Oh my . . ." she said, taking the frame and gazing down at the picture within. Her expression lit up like a Christmas tree in a power surge. "He must feel awful that he missed our appointment. He's trying to make amends!"

"I'm sorry?" said Lucy, looking puzzled.

"Never mind, Ms. Fir," Ms. Snapper said, beaming. "Thank you very much."

Lucy Fir walked away, still looking slightly confused,

and Ms. Snapper stared adoringly at the picture.

The stage door burst open and in strode GG McGee. She wore a powder-blue suit. Her bright green one was likely away having a several-course meal steamed out of it. She carried Molly in a small, expensive-looking gold bag on her right shoulder.

"Please," she said in a trumpeting voice to the nearest stagehand, "inform Dr. Devilish that I need a word with him regarding his *Strange Science* contract as soon as possible. There is a matter of some fine print that needs correcting."

So Dr. Devilish was one of GG's clients as well. No wonder she'd been hanging around the set.

To Fisher's horror, GG spied him.

"Basley! What a lucky coincidence!" She clattered over to Fisher, almost knocking over a light technician. Maybe those sunglasses impaired her peripheral vision after all.

"Uh, yeah," Fisher said. "I'm an admirer of Dr. Devilish's work. I'm studying his show to see if I can incorporate some of his—er—*talent* into my own technique."

"Splendid!" McGee replied. "Have you been thinking about the business matters we discussed at our meeting?"

Fisher felt his classmates' eyes turn in his direction.

"Well," he muttered, "I haven't had too much time to

think about it, but I'll, uh, let you know when I've had a chance to speak to my . . . um, legal team." *Please go away*, he thought. *Please go away.*

"Let me know," McGee said, winking. "There's plenty of work to be done if we want to make our little friend a star. I see a bright future for the both of you, and I want to seize every opportunity that comes to us. . . . Oh my!" She exclaimed suddenly. Then she brought her hands together to make a little square frame, through which she watched FP and Wally the Wombat as they played around. "Just look at that! The chemistry! The character balance! The cinematic potential!"

"I'm sorry?" Fisher said, looking at FP pushing Wally with his snout, trying to get him to leap higher.

"Those two look like they were born for a screen partnership. They could be the next Luke Skywalker and Han Solo."

"If . . . Luke and Han were a pig and a wombat?" Fisher said.

"Exactly," McGee said. "Now you understand."

"I really don't," confessed Fisher, but GG ignored him.

With a series of high-pitched barks, McGee's dog, Molly, hopped out of her bag and joined in the fun, chasing FP and Wally around in circles.

"Look!" GG said, pointing excitedly. "Now we have a Leia, too! Oh, I'm so proud of you, Mollykins!"

"Well, I'll ... give it some thought," said Fisher. "It looks like the taping's about to start."

"Don't take too long," GG said, helping Fisher to herd the playing animals away from the set. "There are plenty of other flying pigs just waiting to take his place." She checked her watch. "Well. It seems our friend Dr. Devilish is too busy at the moment to attend to these *very important matters*," she said in an irritated tone. "So I'm going to step outside and make a few business calls while I wait. I may just see about getting some work for our little friend!" She reached down to pat FP, whose chomping jaws narrowly missed her hand.

Strange Science was getting stranger every day. Dr. Devilish was assembling a heaping pile of plastic tubing and barrel-like chambers on his worktable for the second part of the "Fur Spots and Kilowatts" episode. The class sat restlessly on the audience risers, watching him work. Fisher took his place as Wally, Molly, and FP explored underneath the risers.

"It will take a few moments to finish setting up the equipment," Dr. Devilish trumpeted cheerily.

"Do you need any help?" Ms. Snapper asked, sidling up to his table. "I'd be happy to provide you with any *assistance* you need." She batted her eyelids so fast, it looked like she was trying to create air currents with them.

"Uh ... thank you, but no," Dr. Devilish said. "This

requires a lot of, um, delicate work and precision."

"I promise you, I can be very delicate," Ms. Snapper replied, not budging from his side.

"Sooo!" Dr. Devilish said, swiveling quickly away from Ms. Snapper, who continued to gaze at him longingly. "I think I'll ask the studio audience a question! Who can guess what I'm going to be assembling?"

Fisher wished Dr. Devilish were assembling a giant catapult; then he could use it to shoot himself to the moon.

"It looks kind of like a vacuum cleaner," said Sarah Westbrook, running her many-ringed hand along the pink spikes of her hair.

"Very good!" Dr. Devilish said. "That is exactly what I am creating. For the suction force I'm using this ordinary, household lawn mower engine," he said, lifting up a small motor that had been set into a large, plastic drum. He began outfitting it with various pieces of plastic and rubber tubing. "Now, for the most crucial part—the filter. What if you haven't got one on hand? You may be surprised to find out what you can use instead."

"Ooh, I love surprises," Ms. Snapper said, winking.

"Yes, I'm sure." Dr. Devilish coughed nervously and backed away toward his animal cages, pulling the homemade vacuum with him, casting nervous glances at Ms. Snapper, as though worried she would follow him. He raised his voice to the class again. "Certain animal furs have evolved to be particularly good at picking dust and debris out of the air."

"Oh, Dr. Devilish!" Ms. Snapper clapped her hands together, making her extra-long, beaded earrings jangle. "How do you *know* all of these things?"

Ms. Snapper's eyes were locked on him. Dr. Devilish backed up like a trapped antelope under the watch of a lioness, still struggling to make it through his demonstration.

"Education, Ms. Snapper!" he replied with false cheer. "Beauty is an educational thing. I mean, education is a beautiful thing! Anyway . . ." He cleared his throat and smiled at the audience. "As I was saying! Vacuums! Filters! The rabbit is a creature whose fur is perfectly suited to filter debris. Behold, nature in action!"

He tripped a switch, and the motor came to life. With one hand, he groped behind him. He just missed the rabbit cage and plucked up a raccoon. Before he saw what he was doing, he dropped the animal into a small chamber in the vacuum.

The audience gasped. The machine began sputtering and whining. Fisher could hear the raccoon scrabbling around, clawing and biting at the chamber around it. The vacuum slid forward, then began hopping and bouncing back and forth as the raccoon struggled desperately to escape its plastic prison.

146

The tubes flailed crazily, lashing through the air with frightening speed. Dr. Devilish barely managed to duck and dodge around the vacuum cleaner as it knocked over lighting and sound equipment, sending showers of sparks through the air. Ms. Snapper screamed and had to dive under the table as an out-of-control vacuum arm lashed in her direction, snapping her purse off her shoulder.

The crew rushed in, trying to get close enough to turn the vacuum off, but the flailing rubber arms were spiraling so fiercely, they were forced to take cover.

"Shut it off! Shut it off!"

"It's heading for camera A!"

Microscopes and flasks went sailing through the room as the infernal machine traced a slow path of destruction around Dr. Devilish's lab.

Fisher was so transfixed by the sight of the vacuum and the crowd of people trying to reach it that he didn't notice Amanda had left her seat until he saw her hurtling onto the stage, dive-tackling the vacuum to the floor and pinning it into a wrestling lock. She was able to hold the vacuum's arms long enough for Lucy Fir to jump in and turn it off.

A dizzy raccoon stumbled out of the plastic body, scampering in loops before collapsing.

"Oh, Dr. Devilish!" Ms. Snapper said, rushing to his

side and clutching his arm. "Are you all right?"

"No," he said, taking a deep breath and softly but resolutely prying her arm from his, "but I *will* be, if you would do me the honor of leaving me alone. *Permanently.*" He dusted himself off as Ms. Snapper jerked away from him.

"Thank you!" Dr. Devilish said as he turned to Amanda, who was breathing hard and wiping sweat from her forehead. "You've got some impressive skills. I don't suppose you might be interested in becoming a *Strange Science* assistant, would you?"

Amanda was about to reply when Ms. Snapper stepped in, her forehead creased in a tight frown, her lips drawn thin.

"I remind you, Ms. Cantrell, that we are returning to Wompalog tomorrow," Ms. Snapper said coldly. She glared at Dr. Devilish. "I'm afraid that will be impossible, Dr. Devilish."

"Thanks, Dr. D," Amanda said, shrugging, as Ms. Snapper walked her back to the risers. "But science is my worst subject, anyway."

He leaned in and gave her an exaggerated wink. "Mine too."

A man stumbled toward Fisher. One of the plastic tubes that had been used to construct the vacuum was stuck on his head.

"Mmmrrrff! Mrrrf!" was all that Fisher could hear. Worried that the man might be running out of air, he took a folding chair from nearby, stood on it, and barely managed to pry the plastic tube off. The face of Henry, the ever-troubled sound man, was revealed.

"Henry!" Fisher said. "Are you okay?"

"Yeah, thanks," said Henry, breathing hard. Fisher hopped down from the chair, and Henry collapsed next to him. "You haven't seen Wally running around, have you? We lost track of him."

"A minute ago he was playing with my pig. . . ." Fisher said, trailing off as he looked around. "FP? *FP?*" There was no sign of Fisher's pet anywhere.

"Molly?" At the same moment, GG McGee's high-pitched wail pierced the studio. She dropped to her hands and knees, searching under the risers. "Has anyone seen my Molly??"

Filming shut down completely, as all the crew members of the *Strange Science* show, as well as all the Wompalog students and even Dr. Devilish, conducted a thorough search of the studio. But all three animals had vanished. It was getting late. The crew of *Strange Science* assured Fisher and McGee that they would search the lot and the neighboring lots immediately, and swore that FP and Molly would be found before midnight. And if they weren't found before mid-morning the next day when

How
Dr. Devilish's experiment was SUPPOSED to work

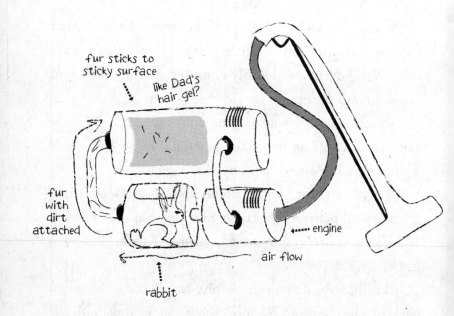

fur sticks to
sticky surface

like Dad's
hair gel?

fur
with
dirt
attached

engine

air flow

rabbit

the class was scheduled to return, they promised to alert the LAPD immediately—a promise that gave Fisher little comfort.

Fisher reluctantly agreed to return to the hotel with the rest of the class, despite feeling nauseous with worry. McGee, teary-eyed, said she would return home, too, to get some rest.

Now there were two people—technically a person and a pig, but Fisher thought of FP as a smaller, pinker person—that Fisher had to find, somewhere in this giant city. And all the while, somewhere out there, somebody else continued to look for *him*. And the longer he took with his finding, the closer he and Two would get to being found.

CHAPTER 14

People threaten to destroy me all the time, so I try to take it as a compliment. If someone threatens to destroy you, they think that you're important. It can actually make you feel kind of special. . . . Unless you get destroyed. Try to avoid that.

—Vic Daring (Issue #45)

At dinner that night, Fisher used his fork to separate the star fries into their separate points, then cutting the points in half, then rearranging them into various geometric patterns on his plate.

He had never believed in karma before. Now, for the first time, he wondered whether he was being punished for creating Two. Fisher had wanted a clone because he wanted to *avoid* attention. Two had been in LA for barely a week, and already he was on the verge of becoming honest-to-God famous. People fawned over him. Older girls swarmed him. Kevin Keels himself stopped to say hello to him. GG McGee acted like she wanted to be his mother.

Meanwhile, Fisher was slowly but surely losing Veronica to a pop singer who didn't even really sing his terrible songs. He was being hunted by spies across the length and breadth of California, and now his best friend in the world—and at this point, probably his *only* friend in the world—had vanished. He knew it would be foolish not to think that FP's disappearance was unrelated to the spies who were pursuing him, but figuring out what to *do* about it was a whole other matter.

One way or another, he was going to have to take action, and he was going to have to do it tonight. He would have to strike out on his own, with no help from Amanda or anyone else. That meant braving the wilds of Los Angeles after dark. At the same time, if the *Strange Science* crew called Ms. Snapper to report that they'd found FP, and Fisher wasn't there, she'd find out that he'd left the hotel without permission and that would make things even worse. He was treading on a narrow ledge above a two-thousand-foot drop.

Even though Fisher hadn't eaten a single bite of the fries and special sauce congealing on his plate, his stomach felt as heavy as a cement block. Now he knew what people spoke about when they said "rock bottom." Things couldn't get any worse. Two could be anywhere. FP could be anywhere.

Fisher wanted to think that the agents after him wouldn't hurt an animal, but if they'd chase a little kid in broad daylight, who knew what their limits were?

And then Kevin Keels strutted through the door, and Fisher's low got 100 percent lower.

A chorus of shouts and cheers filled the room. Keels was surrounded by his usual retinue of followers, managers, bodyguards, and agents screaming into cell phones. GG, Fisher was happy to see, was not among them.

Fisher saw Veronica's eyes light up instantly. As a table was quickly cleared for Kevin across the room, Fisher looked back and forth between the pop star and Veronica, then sighed to himself. He had somehow alienated his only ally, he had lost his clone, and his doom seemed imminent.

It was all over for him. He had failed Two. Sooner or later, the clone's existence would come to light, and he'd be dissected like a bio class frog, and it would be Fisher's fault. And when the secret of Two was discovered, his parents would kill him before the government agency could get to him. Or lock him in a tank with the musical octopus. Which was pretty much the same thing.

The least he could do with the little remaining time he had was to try to make Veronica—beautiful, wonderful, totally out-of-his-league Veronica—happy.

Fisher got up from his seat, walked down the table, and grabbed Veronica's hand. He tried to ignore the shock that the touch alone sent through him.

"Follow me," he said, forcing a smile onto his face. He didn't look back as he led her over to Keels's table.

"Basley, my man," Kevin said as Fisher walked up next to him.

"Hey, Kev," Fisher said, trying to match the singer's cool tone. "I thought I'd introduce you to a friend of mine. This is Veronica." Fisher stepped aside as Veronica, loose-jawed, waved and giggled. "She's got a real way with words," Fisher added. "Might be able to help you out with some lyrics. All right, I'll see you both later."

He turned away, feeling his heart boil away into vapor. Almost instantly, it seemed to recondense into a ten-ton brick. *I know what you are, you lousy fake,* he thought as hard as he could, imagining that Kevin Keels could hear him. *I'm only doing this because it's what she wants. You'd better not let her down.*

"That was quick," Trevor said, walking up to him as he went back to his table.

"What was?" Fisher asked.

"I saw you walk into the bathroom, like, ten seconds ago. Were you just checking out your hair or something?"

"I wasn't in the . . ." Fisher's pulse stopped entirely, then came hammering back like his veins were full of pebbles. *Two.* "Um, yes, actually," he corrected himself, taking a slow step back, then a quicker one. "My hair. I should check it again, in fact." He turned and broke into a full-on sprint.

He shoved the men's room door so hard it cracked a tile on the wall. The noise startled the bathroom's only occupant.

155

Without having to look into the mirror, Fisher was looking at his face.

"You!" Fisher said barely above a whisper.

"Yeah," Two said, his expression hard. "Me. I'm here because we need to have a little talk. I'm tired of your lies."

"What . . . do you mean?" said Fisher. He shot a nervous glance at the door behind him, praying no one would have to use the bathroom.

"Amanda confronted me last night," Two said. "She asked me to come back."

"You *should* come back!" Fisher shouted. "We're very close to being—"

"I'm not done," Two cut in. "I asked her how long she's been fighting our enemies. About what steps she wants to take against Wompalog and its overlords. About the guards and how we might escape them."

"And?" Fisher said, holding his breath and hoping that the next words out of Two's mouth would be anything other than what he expected them to be.

"And she looked at me like I was crazy," Two said, exactly the words Fisher had been dreading he would say. "Oh, she tried to play along after that, but she couldn't cover up her initial reaction. *What* side is she really on? Who are we really fighting?"

"Look," Fisher said, "I told you people were coming after

Early Plans for a
Two-trapping device

convert suitcase to cage

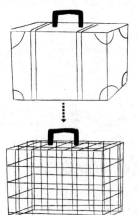

LIST OF POTENTIAL PROBLEMS

1) Likelihood of Two fitting inside

2) Keeping FP out of the trap

3) Being outsmarted by Two

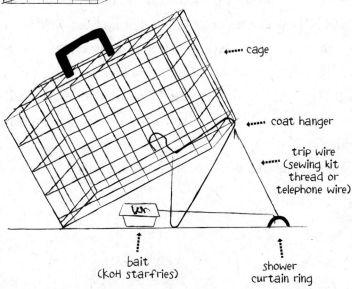

cage ......▶

coat hanger ......▶

trip wire
(sewing kit
thread or
telephone wire) ......▶

bait
(KoH starfries)

shower
curtain ring

us, and now you've seen it for yourself. We can discuss the details after we make a getaway. For now, we need to focus on getting back home without being caught!"

"I'm not going anywhere just yet," Two said, walking past Fisher and putting a hand on the door. "First, I'm going to find out what's going on, with or without your help." With that, Two pulled the door open and stormed out.

"Wait!" Fisher said, on the verge of bolting after him. "This could be our last—" The bathroom door slammed closed an inch from Fisher's nose. Fisher realized what would happen if his classmates saw them both at the same time. Helplessly, he hid in a stall, stewing.

Two was taking matters into his own hands. Fisher would have to do the same. He might be lying to Two, but he was doing it for the sake of both of their lives. Wasn't he? He clenched his fists tightly as he stood up from the stall. He was tired of being followed. He was tired of sneaking around. He was tired of explaining himself to Amanda. But most of all, he was tired of being ignored.

He was out of time. Two was coming home . . . one way or another.

≋ CHAPTER 15 ≋

PEOPLE WONDER WHY I LIKE TO JUST SIT AROUND FOR HOURS AND THINK ABOUT THE UNIVERSE. I WONDER WHY PEOPLE WATCH TV SHOWS WHERE CONTESTANTS RUN THROUGH GIANT LEGO OBSTA-CLE COURSES FOR MONEY. WE'VE ALL GOT OUR MYSTERIES.

—WALTER BAS

Fisher threw the bathroom door open when enough time had passed that he thought it would be safe.

Moving deliberately and with confidence, he strode right out of the King of Hollywood, across the entrance plaza, and onto the sidewalk, moving at a quick pace.

Other hotels and large restaurants dotted the street near the hotel, and Fisher wove through the thick crowds. He had an idea of where Two was staying and felt confident he could track Two down at his home. He didn't know what he was going to do when he got there, but he was getting Two to come back with him if he had to hog-tie him and throw him in a duffel bag.

He would track FP down, too, even if it meant he had to break into every warehouse and basement in Los Angeles to do it.

He still wrestled with the question of what he was

going to do in the long term. The people coming after him weren't going to stop until they either recovered the missing AGH or were satisfied that Fisher wasn't responsible for its loss. There was no more AGH for him to return. The only thing he could think of was keeping Two completely hidden until the agents left his trail. But then what? He couldn't just parade the clone out again. And it really didn't look like Two felt like being a hermit for the rest of his life.

What had Two said? *We can't keep a lid on this thing forever, you know.* Fisher knew that he was right. When he had created Two, he had been thinking only of immediate possibilities and consequences. What would happen in two years, or five years, or ten years? What would happen when Fisher left home to go to college? Could he really expect to keep the world in the dark about Two for that long?

The only other way to maintain the illusion of a single Fisher, was for the original to leave Palo Alto himself. If Fisher-2 wouldn't disappear, then Fisher-1 would have to. But even if the plan had been vaguely appealing, he didn't think it would actually work. His parents were bound to notice the difference.

Which left him the option of telling the truth.

Which brought him right back to the spy problem.

In other words, things would be just as bad as they'd always been.

The King of Hollywood was close to Melrose Avenue, a major boulevard that ran for miles through LA. If he walked it for long enough, he would eventually reach the little spur of Melrose Place, where GG McGee had said he'd be able to find Two.

So he'd walk. He knew that he might be late getting back, but if a lecture from Ms. Snapper was the harshest thing he'd have to face tonight, he'd count it as a giant win. With Two gone renegade and FP kidnapped, he no longer cared about chaperones, schedules, or curfews. Besides, if he failed and his pursuers caught up to him, chances are nobody at Wompalog would ever see him again, let alone be able to send him to detention.

Fisher thrust his hands into his pockets as he walked. His left hand brushed against a piece of paper that was starting to feel old and torn. He pulled it out and unfolded it. The glaring lights of a rodeo-themed barbecue restaurant tinged it a dull red.

It was his sheet of first-kiss calculations. He stopped in his tracks, staring down at the long series of numeric sequences, variables, and multipart equations, which all contributed to the eventual value of the final variable K. K was probably about equal to the number of stars in the sky by this point. Veronica's affection had settled firmly on a pop singer who wasn't even a real singer. Despite the events of the past weeks, Fisher realized

Places I'll be able to live once Two becomes famous:

Mars
the Moon
deserted island (Galápagos?)
adrift on a raft
mountain caves
Antarctica
adrift on an ice floe
government detention facility

nothing had really changed. He was still just as big a nobody as ever.

With shaking hands, he started tearing pieces off the note, one by one, until he had reduced it to a handful of long strips. Then he turned those strips in his hand and kept ripping until it was reduced to tiny squares. He sorted all of the squares into a little stack, and with a final, teeth-gritting twist, turned the note to confetti. He stepped up to the curb and flung it into the street, not caring who was watching or what they thought.

It was only then, in the corner of his peripheral vision, that he realized he *was* being watched. A little ways back, on the other side of the glowing, multicolored Melrose

Avenue, was the black car. He turned to face it, and all four doors started to ease open.

His brain was stuck, unable to process, but his legs took over all by themselves. He bolted along the busy sidewalk, dodging through the crowd, careening around lampposts. Above the noise of the crowd he was just able to make out the sound of quick footsteps not far behind.

Fisher glanced behind him. His black-suited pursuers—three men who were about four times his size, and a woman who was merely three times his size—were having far more trouble dodging through the crowd than he was. People shouted as they were rudely shoved aside. But he knew that they would catch up to him sooner or later.

A thick crowd milled around a doorway to his left, and he wormed his way through it, nearly getting crushed by the sheer pressure of the crowd, his nostrils stinging as a thick blanket of perfume and cologne assaulted them.

He pushed through the crowd, which was packed as tightly as rain forest canopy. Through the muffling wall of people, he felt more than heard a powerful rhythmic thudding and wondered whether he was being pushed toward some kind of construction site. Just like at the Hollywood Bowl, he was so small and the crowd was so bustling and noisy, nobody seemed to notice him. He just slipped through a bunch of legs as quickly as he could, hoping the spies would lose him in the chaos.

All of a sudden, he popped out of the crowd into a strange, dark room lit only with powerful lasers that whirled around in time to the thudding he had heard, which became almost deafening. People were everywhere— mashed up against one another, waving their arms and bobbing back and forth, up and down in time to the skull-bruising pounding.

It was then that Fisher realized where he was: a dance club. For a second, he was hypnotized by the swaying patrons, the shimmering lasers, and the beat that felt like it was being generated inside of his rib cage. But just for a second. Casting a glance behind him, he saw the crowd at the entrance being jostled by his pursuers.

It was only about 9:00 P.M., early for a place like this, and there was enough space in the dance crowd to move through quickly. Unfortunately, that would also make him easier to spot.

A broad, open dance floor dominated the main room. The only places to hide were a handful of pillars near the walls and behind the dancers themselves. Fisher wound his way between the gyrating club-goers, sparing a look back just in time to see the four agents push their way fully into the club. They split up and fanned out, sliding between the dancers.

Fisher slunk behind a pillar, his panic rising. Two agents were combing the crowd clustered against the walls, and two were searching the dance floor. Fisher would be spotted at any second.

He slipped deeper into the room, which was dim with fog from a smoke machine. When he reached the back wall, he started fumbling his way along it, trying to find a back door. He grasped a handle and wrenched a door open, slipping inside.

"Well, if it isn't Fisher!" said a familiar voice.

Fisher looked up, realizing he was in the DJ's booth. The small room was mostly filled with a huge control board sitting behind a fish-tank window that looked out onto the dance floor. And sitting in the rolling chair behind that control board was Henry the sound guy.

"Henry??" Fisher said as the young man listened to one ear of a giant pair of headphones, adjusting a few dials.

"Yeah," he said, "this is my other gig! Not bad, right? Hey, it looks like we've got some newcomers on the floor!"

He adjusted some other controls, and several bright green spotlights popped into focus in the center of the dance floor, where the four agents had regrouped. They looked around, confused, as the other dancers backed up and formed a circle around them, clapping in time to the pulsing beat.

The spies were excellent at maintaining their cover, Fisher had to admit. All four of them broke into dance moves, including spins, synchronized kicks, and *Saturday Night Fever*–style points.

"Man!" said Henry, grooving along in his chair. "These folks have some moves! I wonder who they are?"

"Yeah . . ." said Fisher, shaking his head. "Me too."

The spies kept dancing until Henry turned the spots off. After a few whispered words, they then retreated in the direction they had come. Either they'd decided that Fisher had slipped out during the dance or they didn't want to stick around and draw any more attention to themselves.

"Well," Fisher said, "I should get going. Thanks, Henry."

"For what?" Henry said.

"Oh, um," Fisher wracked his brain for proper terminology, "for, y'know, throwing down, the, uh, freshest, hippest beats?"

"That is what I do, my young friend!" Henry said, turning back to his console. "Rock on!"

Fisher at last found a back way out of the club. For ten minutes, he weaved and twisted along smaller streets and side alleys, just to make sure he'd shaken the spies off his tail.

He was finally beginning to breathe again when he realized he had absolutely no idea where he was. And the more he thought about it, the less likely it seemed that he would be able to find Two, even if he reached Melrose Place. And then there was FP. When he actually took a calm moment to think about it, he saw the enormity of the task before him. Fisher had absolutely no leads on the location of the little pig. He could literally spend years searching this colossal city and never come close.

And on the chance that FP had just run off with the other animals for fun and was found, Fisher wanted to be back at the hotel to receive the news.

Besides, it was clearly too dangerous for Fisher to be out walking the streets with the agents undoubtedly still combing the area for him. He would find his way back to the hotel, and re-strategize once he got there.

He wandered along down the street, looking for a landmark, or a phone booth, or anyone who might help him, but everyone bustled past him without sparing him a second glance. Then, up ahead, he saw a small diner, its simple DINER sign friendly in warm rust-red neon.

He pushed open the glass door, which felt more like it was made of stone, and walked to the counter, taking a seat on a burgundy vinyl-cushioned stool. He had just enough change to buy a Coke. Something sweet might do him some good.

"What'll it be, sweetheart?" said the waitress behind the counter, walking up to him. She had a pretty, kind face and bright blue eyes, with light brown hair pulled up into a bun.

"I'll just have a . . ." The rest of Fisher's sentence dried up in his mouth as he looked at her more closely. He *knew* that face. "You . . ." he said, his eyes expanding out in all directions. "You're the woman from the Spot-Rite commercials!"

"Get your spots right out," she said in a tired, sarcastic version of her commercial voice. "Yep, that's me. *Was* me. I got let go when the company decided to go in another direction with its ad campaign. Luckily, I've got another gig lined up that'll be starting soon, so I can get out of this place. My name's Jenny." She tapped the plastic name tag on her worn-looking uniform with her fingernail. "Jenny Nichols." She extended her hand.

"Fisher Bas," Fisher said, shaking her hand, awed. Here she was. The woman who Two believed was his mother. And all the while, Two was trying to work his way into the Spot-Rite ads, thinking it would bring him closer to her. But here she was, serving up diner grub for a few dollars in tips.

"So what are you doing here all by yourself?" Jenny said, turning around to use the soda fountain. She set a tall glass of Coke down in front of Fisher. "On the house. You look like you could use it."

"Wow . . . thank you," Fisher said, grabbing the straw

and taking a long sip. The ice-cold soda rushed down his throat, giving him a mild brain-freeze. It was exactly what he needed.

"Are your parents nearby? Haven't you got homework to do or something?"

"Well, I . . ." Fisher paused, looked down, and sighed. If nothing else, he could at least tell the truth to *one* person today. At least part of it. "I came here on a school trip. We're staying at the big King of Hollywood hotel. I wandered away and got lost."

"Well," she said, "it just so happens that my shift ends in a few minutes. Stick around, relax, drink up. I'll give you a ride when I'm done."

"Thank you," Fisher said, resting his head on his hand. It had been the most exhausting two days of his life—and given some of his days lately, that was saying something. He rubbed his face with both hands, trying to release some of the built-up stress. He took slow, deep breaths, and his sprinting brain gradually slowed to a jog, and then a walk. He would find his way out of this. He just had to keep calm, think, and determine the best course of action. His breathing began to relax even more. The coldness in his head broke apart. . . . Now he felt warm. . . .

"Have a good nap?"

Fisher looked up in surprise. Two was sitting on the

stool next to him. Jenny Nichols was gone. Everyone else was gone.

"Two!" Fisher said. "How did you find me?"

"I have my ways," Two said, smiling. "Come here, let me show you what I found." Two grabbed Fisher's hand and led him to the back of the dining area, to the kitchen door.

"You found something in the kitchen?" Fisher asked, puzzled.

"You'll see," Two replied, and they walked in.

Fisher looked around.

"Wow," he said. "This looks exactly like our kitchen at home. So what was it that you found?"

"This." Two frowned and pointed to a dark, circular stain on the counter. "It's a spot. It's been driving me crazy. I'm going to have to get it right out." With that, he pulled a small-sized bottle of Spot-Rite from his pocket, poured it out over the spot, grabbed a cloth, and began scrubbing. The spot didn't come out immediately, and he scrubbed faster and faster, until his arm was almost a blur. Fisher thought he smelled a faint hint of smoke.

"Be careful," Fisher said.

"I have to get this spot out!" Two said more urgently, working even faster.

The counter began smoking and crackling.

"Two, stop! It's too hot!" Fisher shouted. But it was too late. Sparks flew across the room, and trails of fire began *to spread along the floor, lapping at the walls.*

"Oh, no!" Two said. "I have to call for help!" He ran to a window and started shouting for help. Fisher noticed that the window looked out on a large city street, and they were about ten stories up. But Two's screams were drowned out by the sound of trumpets and pounding drums.

"Look!" Two said excitedly as the flames closed in behind him. "There he is!"

"Who?" Fisher said. "Where's that music coming from??"

With that, Two climbed out the window and jumped.

Fisher leapt forward with a terrified cry, only to find that Two hadn't fallen to his death. He was sitting proudly on top of . . . FP. Only FP was the size of a cart horse, float-ing in midair, and wearing a red spandex suit with a giant black A on his belly.

"It's Ace McSnout!" Two called. "That daring, dashing do-gooder whose delightful deeds deliver the decent from doom! Come on, Fisher! Jump!"

Fisher's eyes were watering. The flames were practically at his back now. He could hardly breathe.

"Jump, Fisher! Jump! Fisher!!"

"Fisher."

Fisher woke up with a start. Jenny was shaking him gently. "Wake up. You nodded off."

Fisher opened his eyes. The cold counter gently squashed his cheek. He sat up, shaking his head, trying to clear the bizarre dream from his mind. It had felt so real. . . . He shivered. He could almost feel the heat of the flames on his back.

"Thank you," Fisher said, rubbing his eyes.

"It's no problem, Fisher. Let's get you back to your hotel."

The image of FP as a giant superhero was lodged in Fisher's head. He felt a lump swell in his throat. He didn't know where the little pig had run off to, but he prayed he was safe. And he wished that even now, Ace McSnout was on his way to swoop up Fisher and Two and save the day.

≋ CHAPTER 16 ≋

I've heard a lot of people talk about trying to find them-selves. I don't think this is what they meant.

—Fisher Bas, Personal Notes

Fisher padded quietly down the hotel hallway, locked in the hazy realm between total exhaustion and racing anxiety. He reached his door just as the footsteps of the chaperone on late patrol echoed in the stairwell. He jabbed his card key into its slot, opening the door as quickly and quietly as he could and letting it shut behind him gently.

Fisher didn't want to turn the lights on, so he stood in place for a minute until his eyes adjusted. Warren was asleep, tucked entirely under the covers. Fisher tiptoed to his bed, pulled the covers back and, without bothering to change, crawled beneath them, letting out a long breath as his head dropped to the pillow.

He felt something crunch slightly under his head. Warren had probably been eating chips in Fisher's bed. He sat up, annoyed, feeling for the offending object.

It wasn't a chip. It was a piece of paper, and it was taped in place on the pillow.

Fisher's sleepiness quickly melted away. With a trembling hand, he flicked on the bedside lamp.

The note was written on plain white paper in thick, black pen and neat, angular block letters: *Come to Studio Lot 44 at midnight if you ever want to see Two or the pig alive again.*

Fisher's breathing stopped. Then it seemed to race forward, until it sputtered triple time. He brought the note closer, as though that might somehow change what was written there. But the same evil words glared up at him.

Fisher sprang from his bed, note in hand. No longer remembering to be quiet, he raced into the hall and down to Amanda's door. He rapped on the door with his knuckles. When there was no reply, he rapped a little harder.

The door opened slowly. As Fisher had feared, Amanda had obviously been sleeping. Her face was crinkly, and she squinted in response to the bright hallway light. Surprisingly, her pajamas were pink. Fisher had assumed Amanda would sleep in body armor or something.

"Fisher?" she said tiredly. "What do you want?"

He handed her the note. "I found this on my pillow just now." He watched as she read it, and her puzzlement turned to genuine fear. Fisher's heart galloped up to panic velocity.

"FP and Two are clearly in danger." *Again,* he added

COME TO STUDIO LOT 44
AT MIDNIGHT IF YOU
EVER WANT TO SEE TWO
OR THE PIG ALIVE AGAIN

silently. "Look, I *have* to go to Studio Lot 44. Will you help me?"

For a second, Amanda looked like she was going to say no. She turned away from Fisher, so he could only see her profile. Then she sucked in a deep breath and said, with a toss of her hair, "Two may be a loudmouthed, stuck-up, wannabe movie star, but he at least deserves to live to see his first birthday. And I won't let anything happen to FP. I'll get a few things together. Meet me in the hallway stairwell in five minutes." She vanished back into her room and closed the door too fast for Fisher to respond. He raced back to his own room. All of his exhaustion had burned away.

Exactly five minutes later, he was standing in the hallway again, his prototype Shrub-in-a-Backpack slung over his left shoulder, packed with every useful and semi-useful device he could find in his suitcase.

Amanda was already waiting. She was wearing gray jeans, a black turtleneck, and well-worn athletic shoes. In place of her glasses was a sleek pair of prescription athletic goggles. She cracked her knuckles and nodded at Fisher.

"Ready to go?" she asked.

"Let's do it," Fisher answered.

Amanda went first, gliding down the hallway without a sound and scouting for any snooping chaperones before slowly pushing open the stairwell door. Fisher followed, trying to keep his sneakers from squeaking.

They reached the lobby. A late-night crowd had gathered, milling around the hotel bar. The stairway was on one side of the large main hall between the front doors and the elevators. Across the hall was the carpeted lounge that led to the restaurant entrance.

"Hang on," Amanda said, raising a hand. She took two hesitating steps out of the stairwell door and glanced around the lobby quickly before returning to Fisher. "Mr. Dubel's sitting in one of the armchairs in the lounge section. We'll need to be careful."

"Maybe there's another way out?" Fisher said. Amanda shook her head.

"I see my ride," she said. "Keep up if you can." She pushed open the door and stepped out into the hall. Fisher followed her hastily, just as a full luggage trolley rolled from the elevators toward the doors. Amanda scooted beside it, matching her pace to its motion. The towers of suitcases and duffel bags concealed her entirely from view of the lounge. Fisher leapt behind her, and they made it out the front doors without being spotted.

"It's ten thirty. If we walk briskly we'll just make it to the studio lots," Amanda said, checking her watch.

Fisher was trying to remember the layout of the studio lots. "*Strange Science* is on Studio Lot 43. *Keel Me Now* was next door on 42. So what's on Studio Lot 44?"

"I guess we'll find out," Amanda said grimly.

Fisher's bag strap jostled up and down on his shoulder with every quick step. Amanda was two paces in front of him, moving briskly and in silence. The blare of horns and the screech of car traffic sounded distant, like alarms heard from underwater.

They passed rows of stores that seemed miles long. Patrons at a sidewalk café gave them curious but brief looks as they passed. Fisher's eyes constantly scanned the road for any sign of the black car.

Two had been alive for less than a month. In that time he had been kidnapped, threatened with torture and death, had narrowly escaped vaporization in the explosion of TechX, and had been saved only by some ingenuity and a massive lucky break. Now, it seemed, he'd been abducted all over again, and could be in equal or even greater danger.

All in the space of a few weeks.

When Fisher had been making Two, he had thought of the clone entirely as a tool. A machine, like any of the gadgets in his lab, intended to serve a specific purpose. It had never really crossed his mind before Two came to life that the clone would truly *have* a life.

Fisher felt a sharp stab of guilt. He remembered what the evil Dr. X had said to him just before the explosion at TechX: *we're not so different, you and me.*

Could Dr. X have been right?

Fisher pushed the thought out of his mind as they passed into the massive complex of studio lots, their foot-steps faint on the asphalt. Only a few security lights illuminated the area. There were no guards in sight. Fisher wondered if someone had deliberately arranged for the lot to be emptied, and shivered.

Then: a new light clicked on in the distance. Fisher and Amanda both jumped a foot in the air. A small lamp protruded from of the side of the main studio structure, directly above a red side door.

"I guess that's our invitation," Amanda said. Fisher thought she sounded nervous, but she kept walking.

Even though Fisher's legs felt leaden, it seemed that all too soon, he and Amanda had crossed the distance to the building. Above them were the blinking lights of a low-flying plane, and Fisher found himself wishing he were on it. He would rather be anywhere else but here—in this vacant lot, approaching a mysterious door.

Amanda took a deep breath and eased the door open.

The inside of the building was very dark, and they were just able to make out a narrow hallway. Amanda gestured for Fisher to follow her, and they began making their way down the dim corridor. Gradually, the environment grew more claustrophobic; Fisher sensed that the walls were pressing him from either side.

Then the hallways dumped them suddenly into an enormous open space. A few low lights burned high in the vast ceiling above their heads and, in the half light, Fisher could just see an immense soundstage cluttered and stacked with what looked like heaps and mounds of scrap metal and junk, many of them nearly the size of a house.

Amanda came to an abrupt halt, and Fisher almost crashed into her. She drew him into a crouch.

"What?" he whispered into her ear.

"Movement to our left," she whispered, and then held her breath for a moment. "*And* right."

Barely visible figures—no more than looming

shadows—emerged from the darkness: two from the left, one from the right. Henchmen?

Midget henchmen? The figure on the right was very small.

"Hello?" a man's voice called out. It sounded familiar.

"Who . . . who are you?" called the small person on the right, and Fisher found himself even more bewildered than he had been. This voice he definitely recognized. It was Kevin Keels.

Keels stepped into a pool of light. Amanda let out a yelp of surprise.

"Kevin?" said the third person, stepping forward. It was GG McGee. The man with her was Dr. Devilish.

"*What* is going on??" said Amanda, losing her patience and climbing to her feet. Kevin Keels nearly fell over backward in surprise, and Dr. Devilish jumped behind GG McGee, who froze, eyes wide. She had what looked like a bucketful of mascara running down her face.

"You!" Dr. Devilish said. "You're the kid that tackled the vacuum."

"Basley?" chorused GG and Keels together as Fisher stepped forward.

"What are you doing here?" Fisher demanded to no one in particular.

"I received a threatening note," said Dr. Devilish, looking around the room and squinting confusedly. "I was told that if I didn't show up here, now, I'd be exposed."

"Exposed as what?" said Amanda, furrowing her brow.

Even in the darkness, Dr. Devilish's blush was visible. "What I meant to say is . . . my latest top secret *research* would be exposed," Dr. Devilish said quickly, and coughed. "I've been working on a revolutionary new . . . protein, uh, sympathizer."

"You mean synthesizer?" Fisher raised an eyebrow.

"Right, of course," Dr. Devilish said quickly. "A nervous slip of the tongue."

GG McGee cut in. "My note said that they'd taken my little Molly!" she wailed, clenching her teeth as new tears began to form in the corners of her eyes. "And that I'd never see her again unless I showed up! She's so young! She has a career of stardom and glory ahead of her! I can't imagine going on without her!" As she began to sob, Dr. Devilish offered her a few weak pats on the back. "I bumped into Dr. Devilish as we were walking in," she said, regaining control. "I almost knocked his teeth out with my handbag."

"Messing around in the *Strange Science* lab has made me very good at ducking," he replied with a shallow smile, trying to lighten the mood.

"What about you?" Fisher said, looking hard at Keels.

"Oh, uh," he started, reaching up and scratching the

back of his head, "the note threatened blackmail. . . ." A whine crept into his voice, and he looked nervously at GG McGee. Fisher saw her give him a minute shake of the head.

"That's ridiculous," GG said forcedly. "You have nothing to hide."

"No, no, of course not," Kevin stammered eagerly. "I . . . really don't have any idea what the note meant. I came here to find out."

Fisher's eyes burned into Keels's. He knew *exactly* what Kevin's secret was. The only thing that kept him from pressing the pop singer to reveal the truth was the fact that he had an even bigger secret of his own.

"How about you, Basley?" Keels asked as if on cue.

He felt Amanda suck in a breath next to him.

"I . . . like to conduct scientific experiments in my off time," Fisher said. "One of them produced some . . . embarrassing results. I'd rather not have those results be public." Fisher was getting very good at the not technically lying game.

"Who could have brought us here?" said McGee, looking around at the cluttered soundstage. "Who would be so heartless as to kidnap poor Molly?"

"And what in the world *is* this place?" Dr. Devilish demanded.

Before anyone could answer, a heavy series of clanks

gave them a half second's warning before the lights blazed into full force. Fisher's vision went temporarily white.

Then, as his eyes adjusted, he found himself surrounded by reasons to wish the lights had just stayed off.

≋ CHAPTER 17 ≋

Calm your hearts, my friends. This is not the proper time to panic.

> —*Hal Torque, brief sidekick of Vic Daring, moments before being eaten by a space monster*

Fisher felt like he had stepped into a huge, gleaming nightmare. With hisses and creaks, undercut by the bass thrum of huge, electric motors, the soundstage began to unfold.

No. To *rebuild*.

There was the whirring of servos and the muted scream of metal scraping metal, and what had looked like huge piles of junk became, instead, towering mechanized monsters.

Metal trees—thirty feet tall with razor wire–lined branches that whipped from side to side like the brushes of a demonic car wash—ringed the area where they were standing, extending into the distance as far as the eye could see, a forest of deadly steel. Rubber vines slithered along the ground, each studded with barbs whose tips were coated in a sickly green fluid. Giant, metal Venus flytraps sprang up from the ground, snapping their four-foot-wide jaws with bone-severing crashes.

Robotic monsters prowled between the deadly metallic plants. A mechanical Tyrannosaur stalked among the trees, swinging its car-sized head from side to side and searching out prey with glowing ruby-colored eyes. Anacondas made of dozens of flexing titanium segments rolled and slid through the branches, waiting for the right victim to walk beneath them to be smothered in thick, chrome-plated coils.

There were human-looking robots as well, running around on legs or rolling on wheels, weaponry sprouting from arms and torsos. They had a strangely familiar look to them, but Fisher was too terrified to figure out why. His brain screamed at him to run, to run anywhere. But there was nowhere to run. The machines weren't closing in yet, but Fisher didn't imagine they had much time.

All five members of the group—GG, Dr. Devilish, Kevin, Amanda, and Fisher—automatically formed a tight circle. Fisher was surprised to realize that he had instinctively balled up his fists. Since when did he have a fight—and not just a *flight*—instinct?

"What . . . *is* this??" Dr. Devilish managed to squeak out.

"I—I saw commercials for this." Fisher was surprised he could still form a complete sentence. "It's that new reality show: *Sci-Fi: Survivor.* It's a giant obstacle course. Contestants have to solve puzzles and fight their way to the end. But—but the commercials made it look easy. Rubber darts. Pools of foam. This isn't right."

"How big is this place?" Amanda squeaked.

A faint crackle cut through the background hum of machinery.

"I wouldn't concern myself with such trivial questions, if I were you," a man's voice boomed over loudspeakers, making everyone jerk with surprise. "This place is exactly as big as it needs to be for my purposes."

Everyone turned to look at one another.

"Oh," the voice went on cheerfully as the robotic monsters continued to circle and prowl, "I'm sorry, I haven't introduced myself. I am the Producer. I brought you all here. Let me get you up to speed: put simply, you're going to have a romp through my little playground, and I'm going to watch. And probably laugh a great deal."

"Why should we?" Amanda shouted up into the air. "Who are you? What do you want with us?"

"To answer your questions in reverse order," the Producer said, "my reasons are none of your business, knowing my identity won't help you, and you will do what I say because if you don't, you'll all die. Of course, you will very likely die, anyway, but you *certainly* will if you refuse to cooperate. I have not yet given my . . . *creations* the order to attack. You have thirty seconds before I do."

"There's a—there's a dinosaur staring at me," Dr. Devilish croaked.

"Some wheelie thing has me in its sights," said Amanda, her voice rising in panic, tugging on Fisher's sleeve. He followed her panicked gaze. The robot looked like a motorcycle, but with a curved plastic chassis where its driver should be. A single, glaring blue eye stared Amanda down.

"Ten seconds," said the Producer.

The trees began shivering and shaking, branches thrashing in the air. The flytraps clapped their jaws together like castanets.

"Hold still," muttered Fisher urgently. "Nobody move until I say go. Then scatter, okay?"

"Got it," Amanda said.

"Right," said Dr. Devilish. GG McGee whimpered something that sounded like a yes.

"Kevin?" Fisher said. "Did you hear me? *Kevin!*"

"Y-y-y-yess," Keels managed to splutter.

"Five, four, three, two . . . one," the Producer said. A harsh laugh exploded through the speakers. For a second, Fisher felt an idea skirt the edge of his consciousness. . . . The laugh sounded familiar, too. . . .

But he had no time to mull it over.

The Tyranno-bot began to stomp forward, its body

swaying low to the ground. The wheel-bot gunned its engine. Its tires squealed as it sped at Amanda.

"Not yet," Fisher said.

"Fisher . . ." Amanda said nervously.

"Not yet . . ." Fisher said.

"Basley!" GG screeched.

"Not yet . . ." Fisher forced himself to stay rooted in his spot.

The mechanical dinosaur's mouth yawned open, revealing rows of serrated steel teeth. The motorcycle raced forward, gunning to full speed . . . five feet away . . . four . . .

"NOW!" Fisher shouted as he dove and tumbled forward. All five of them scattered in different directions, and the speeding motorcycle collided with the Tyranno-bot, shearing its control capsule off on the dinosaur's teeth. Its sparking wheeled body sped right into the dinosaur's legs, clipping them out from under it. The Tyranno-bot crashed heavily to the ground. Smoke and sparks began to spray from both machines.

"All right," Amanda cried, panting, over the noise of the other machines. "What now? Which way should we go?"

Before anyone could answer, a fuzzy pink blur zipped out of the trees, shot between Fisher's legs and off into the mechanical wilderness.

"FP!" Fisher shouted, bolting after him. The

DIAGRAM OF TYRANNO-BOT

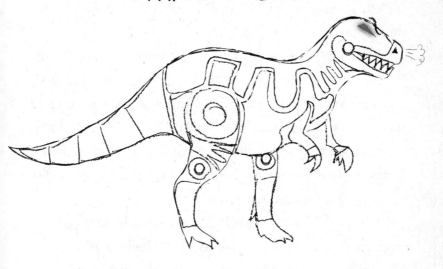

others followed behind him, calling his name—"Fisher!" "Basley!"—and dodging swiping, bladed tree branches and twisting electrical vines.

FP was charting his own course, scurrying ahead in a panic, weaving between the deadly animatronics. Fisher didn't know how he'd escaped, but given the little guy's heroic deeds at TechX, he was hardly surprised. Maybe he was trying to lead them to Two and Molly.

An enormous android stepped out from behind a tree, each arm sprouting a ten-foot whip. Fisher stopped short, and his companions skidded to a halt around him.

The android advanced on them, cracking its whips in

turn. FP had paused ahead of them, whimpering and shaking.

"Oh no, oh no, oh no . . ." Keels said over and over again.

"Shut up," snapped Amanda. "Everybody spread out. We need to give it multiple targets." When nobody moved, she said impatiently, "Listen, I know what I'm doing. I watch a lot of action movies—ahhh!" No sooner had she pronounced the words before a whip lashed itself three times around her waist, pinning her arms to her sides and dragging her off her feet.

"Amanda!" Fisher yelled. The other whip snapped out in a fluid motion, wrapping around Keels and pinning him to the ground. The pop star squealed in terror.

The robot began to pace backward, dragging its two victims along the floor with it.

"Come on!" Fisher rushed forward.

He grabbed hold of the whip that had encircled Amanda, wrapping both arms around it. The whip was made of thick but flexible steel. Fisher couldn't hope to uncoil it. But Fisher's added weight made the android falter for a moment. It gave Fisher an idea. "Devilish, grab the other whip!"

Dr. Devilish shook visibly, but he took two big steps forward and grabbed hold of the whip encircling the whimpering Keels and leaned backward. He was much larger than Fisher, and the added resistance stopped the robot short.

"It's stuck!" Fisher cried. "We're too heavy!" He looked around wildly. "Turn it left! . . . *Left,* Doctor, *left! Your* other *left.*"

With Fisher pulling one way and Dr. Devilish pulling the other, they were able to turn the struggling android. A few feet behind its back were the snapping jaws of a flytrap. "GG, *push!*"

McGee took a few slow, halting steps forward, then planted her hands on the android's body and added her effort to Fisher's and Devilish's.

"This . . ." she began, gritting her teeth and starting to push, as Fisher and Dr. Devilish pulled, "is . . ." The android was forced to take a step back to stay on its feet, then two. "For . . ." Fisher strained with all the strength in his barely one-hundred-pound body. *"Molly!"*

With a final shove from McGee, the android fell backward into the open jaws of the flytrap. The flytrap snapped shut, and a horrible crunching sound filled the air. The flytrap sparked and hissed as the android's body was severed clean from its legs. The whips went slack, and Amanda, who had been fighting and straining all along, burst out of the loose grip. Kevin Keels lay still.

"Kevin!" GG cried out, falling to his side.

"Is he dead?" Devilish asked, his eyes wide. "Badly hurt?"

"No," GG said, "just fainted." She tapped her palm

against his cheek a few times. "Kevin! Kevin! Wake up! That's a good boy."

"I had the most awful dream," Keels said, sounding groggy. "I dreamed that we were trapped in this horrible death maze that . . ." He sat up and looked around. *"Aaauugh!"* As if someone had unplugged him, he instantly passed out again, flopping flat on his back.

Fisher had immediately darted over to FP and had scooped up his pet pig.

"I was worried about you, boy," he said.

FP frantically nuzzled his face and even began to chew on Fisher's ear, which Fisher assumed—rightly—was an expression of happiness. GG struggled to revive her pop sensation client until finally Kevin staggered to his feet again.

A dull, rhythmic popping sound suddenly filled the air. After a moment Fisher realized that it was the sound of someone clapping slowly into a microphone.

"Well done," the Producer's voice rang out. "Very noble and extremely thrilling. I'm sure your audience agrees."

"Audience?" Amanda wrinkled her nose. "We're not actually being *filmed* right now, are we?"

Fisher heard a dull crackling behind him and turned around.

"Uh, guys . . ." he said. "The audience is behind us. . . ."

The others turned. Dozens of fiendish machines had gathered in a rough semicircle behind them. Some had barrel-shaped bodies perched on two thick legs, with spherical heads sprouting antennae. There were more dinosaur-bots, in the shapes of Stegosaurs, Triceratops, and smaller birdlike beasts, all of them with strips of plastic imitation skin covering parts of their bodies, but with metal plating and exposed wires everywhere else. There were robots on wheels, treads, two legs, three legs, and four legs.

"RUN!" Amanda screamed.

Nobody needed to be told twice. The group tore off through the artificial foliage, ducking and weaving between the plants as the troupe of robots stomped after them in hot pursuit.

"Over there!" Dr. Devilish panted out. "Look!"

Fisher whipped his head around to see where Devilish was pointing. There was what looked like a small cement building up ahead, with a door just visible in its side. They ran for it, and Devilish heaved the metal door open, herding the others inside before slamming and bolting the door shut behind him.

They were plunged into pitch darkness. Everything was quiet except for the faint, muffled hums and whirrs of the machines outside and the frantic sounds of their own breathing.

A panel in the ceiling lit up, washing the small cement room in buttery yellow light.

"Well," GG said, patting down her hair. "That wasn't too bad. We'll just stay in here until someone notices we're missing and comes for help."

Kevin was blubbering. "I—I want to go home."

"Quiet," Amanda said sharply. "We'll just have to wait here, like GG said. At least we're safe."

Then there was a *click*. Then another. Finally, a steady, slow *click-click-click* filled the room.

"I don't want to alarm anyone," Dr. Devilish said in a high, trembling voice, "but has anyone else noticed that the ceiling is getting lower?"

CHAPTER 18

My mistake. This is actually the ideal time to panic. If there were a "panic" spot on the clock, both hands would be right smack on it. It is panic past panic o'clock.

—Hal Torque, brief sidekick to Vic Daring, even fewer moments before being eaten by a space monster

FP ran in a circle, feeling his way around the walls. The door they had bolted wouldn't *unbolt*, and there were no other exits.

Everyone was shouting at once, running around in the tiny space. Dr. Devilish and Kevin Keels crashed into each other, and the smaller Keels nearly flipped over backward, smacking into the wall. As he slid onto the ground, shaking his head dizzily, a panel in the wall was dislodged, revealing a small computer screen.

"Hey!" Keels cried out. "Look at this. It's some kind of control panel. . . ." He squinted at it. "There's a weird math problem on the screen. . . ."

"Let me," Fisher said, pushing him out of the way as the ceiling crept downward. His heart jerked with every *click*.

"It's not a math problem," Fisher said. "It's a chemical equation."

The question was fairly straightforward stoichiometry, and Fisher felt a surge of triumph: he knew the
answer. Stoichiometry was what he'd been reviewing
with Mr. Granger just before the teacher had revealed
himself as Dr. X. Fisher did some quick calculations in
his head and tapped in the answer on the keyboard. The
terminal made a pinging sound, and a second question
appeared.

"Looks like lyrics to one of your songs, Kevin," Fisher
said. "With a bunch of blank spots."

Fisher got out of the way as Kevin Keels crouched down
and filled in the blanks as fast as he could. Dr. Devilish
could no longer stand up straight. The room was getting
stuffier and hotter, and Fisher felt the sweat running
down his back.

"Okay!" Keels said. "It's, uh . . . it's a question about
fashionable canine ortho . . . orthodontitis . . ."

"Orthodontics," Fisher corrected him.

"Dog braces?" Amanda piped up. "They make those?"

"Out of my way," GG McGee said, almost throwing
herself down to the keyboard. She took a few seconds to
parse through the question before her hands flew over the
keyboard, landing on the keys like a hard rain. "Done!
Now what's this? . . . A question about different varieties
of hair gel!"

Dr. Devilish dropped from his knees to his stomach

and read through the questions. Fisher was hunched over already when he felt the ceiling touch the back of his neck. He went down to his knees, his breathing getting shallower.

"Please hurry, please hurry," said Keels, lying on his back, his eyes frozen on the ceiling as it descended. Fisher felt the ceiling brush against his hair and went down to his stomach.

"Please shut up so I can concentrate," Dr. Devilish replied. He took a deep breath, and hammered the keyboard like he was trying to tattoo his answer into it.

Fisher's eyes were shut tight, his arms wrapped around FP.

The clicking stopped.

He opened his eyes as the ceiling retreated upward. Then a portion of the wall shuddered downward like a drawbridge, revealing an open path through the forest.

Dazed, they ventured carefully out into the open, eyes darting back and forth, searching for movement. But the robots had either given up the chase or were deep in hiding.

Fisher's mind was spinning. He thought about the computer panel and its series of questions. "A test," he said grimly. "There was a test for each of us. Whoever this guy is, he knows a lot about us. He must have been watching us for years. . . ."

"Why wasn't I tested?" Amanda said.

"Because you weren't supposed to be here," Fisher said. An awful coldness settled in the pit of his stomach. Amanda had almost been squeezed to death by an android, slashed to pieces by steel trees, and crushed to pulp by the trap room—all because he'd asked her to come with him.

As though sensing what he was thinking, Amanda reached out and put a hand on his shoulder. "It's not your fault," she whispered. He managed a faint smile in her direction.

Cautiously, the group advanced along a trail cut conveniently into the artificial wilderness, until they reached a thirty-foot-deep chasm that stretched along in both directions.

"Welcome to my moat," boomed out the unseen Producer, making everybody jump.

"Aren't moats supposed to have water in them?" Amanda shouted, struggling to look defiant.

"When you fall thirty feet onto solid steel, the water isn't really necessary, except perhaps to clean up the mess," the Producer replied in an amused voice. "As you may have noticed, I have recalled my little . . . *friends* for the time being."

Fisher thought of the army of metal monsters and shivered.

"Your next challenge is to get across the moat," continued the Producer. "But I'm warning you—the patience of my little creations won't last forever, so I'd get on with it."

They looked across the gap. It was more than half as wide as it was deep—more than wide enough to stop even the most reckless person from attempting to jump it. Both sides of the chasm were lined with smaller trees that appeared to be mere scenery; thankfully, they weren't outfitted with blades or whirling branches.

Fisher felt FP tugging on him by a dangling backpack strap.

"Not now, boy," he said. "I'm trying to figure out how to get across." FP tugged more insistently. "Seriously, FP, now is not the . . ." he trailed off. "My bag!" He unslung his backpack from his shoulders, and rifled through its contents.

"Thanks, boy. You're more helpful than I give you credit for." FP snorted and looked as pleased with himself as a pig could look.

"Amanda?" Fisher said excitedly. "I think I can get us across the gap, but I'll need your help."

"As usual," she replied. Fisher was about to issue a new string of apologies, but when he looked up he saw a small, teasing smile on her face. "What's the plan?"

Fisher pulled his stretch necktie out of the bag. "This will serve as a zip line," he said. "We can stretch it from one side of the moat to the other. But first somebody needs to cross. That's where *these* come in." He pulled out his specially engineered socks. "They'll absorb the shock of the fall and let you jump-bounce to the other side. . . . I'd do it, but I'm not very athletic," he added apologetically.

"That's an understatement," Amanda said, rolling her eyes. She was already pulling off her own shoes and socks and tugging on the jump-socks.

Fisher and Dr. Devilish tied one end of the necktie securely to a tree, and Amanda took the other end in her hand. With a simple nod and no hesitation, she leapt into the pit. She landed squarely on her feet. The socks absorbed the force of the fall and redirected it into the steel floor so that Amanda was catapulted upward. She landed neatly on the other side. Working quickly, she located another tree and tied it off.

"Wow," Dr. Devilish said. "Nice socks."

"Thanks," Fisher said. "After a while, I got tired of always having to ask someone to reach the tall shelves for me."

"Now what?" GG said. "Do you expect us to shimmy across?"

"Nope," Fisher said. "I expect us to slide." With that, he pulled the bow-tie version of his stretchy ties from his bag.

"What's that?" Keels asked.

"Style," Fisher said as Dr. Devilish nodded approvingly. "Or at least, it was, at some point in history. But it's also strong enough to hold us."

He bit his lip and drew Dr. Devilish a little ways away from the others. "Do you want to double-check my weight calculations?" he asked in a low voice.

"Your . . . ?" Dr. Devilish shook his head. "I . . . uh . . . I'm afraid . . . well, contractually speaking . . ." He took a deep breath. "Look, kid, I can't calculate my way out of the checkout line at a grocery store. I'm . . . I'm not a scientist." He let out a long sigh. "Never have been. In fact, I'm not even a decent actor. I got this *Strange Science* gig because of my looks—and my dazzling smile." He flashed his famous smile at the group, and Fisher had to admit, it *was* impressive. Then his face fell again. "This gig is all I have. Please don't tell anyone."

Dr. Devilish looked so earnest, Fisher couldn't even be angry with him. "Your secret's safe with me," he said, and Dr. Devilish looked relieved. Then Fisher turned back to the rest of the group. "Okay, guys. We'll just have to risk it. I'll go first."

He put his bag back on, put FP into it, tied the bow tie around the necktie, took hold of it with both hands, and

Blueprints for
STRETCH
NECK TIE

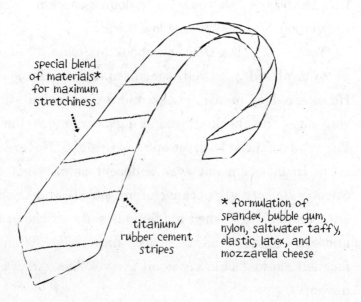

special blend
of materials*
for maximum
stretchiness

titanium/
rubber cement
stripes

* formulation of
spandex, bubble gum,
nylon, saltwater taffy,
elastic, latex, and
mozzarella cheese

with a running jump, slid across the chasm on the make-shift zip line. When he reached the other side he turned and sent the bow tie hurtling back.

Keels crossed next, blubbering and moaning the whole time. Dr. Devilish was preparing to make his crossing when a motion to Fisher's right made him whip around.

He squinted into the foliage, he felt his hair stand up as he saw, or thought he saw, his own eyes looking back at him.

"Two?" he said, stepping forward. "Two, is that you?" But the leaves closed in, and the eyes vanished.

"Did you see that?" he asked Amanda.

"See what?" She frowned at him.

He shook his head. Maybe he'd been seeing things.

A piercing scream cut through the air. Fisher turned to see that the tie had come unknotted from the far side of the chasm. GG, the last to cross, was dangling from one end of the tie, shrieking and kicking, gripping the necktie for dear life. The fall wouldn't kill her, but she could easily break an ankle or an arm, and any injury in this death maze could prove fatal to the whole party. Fisher hurried over and helped Amanda and Dr. Devilish hoist her up as Kevin Keels stood behind them, quivering and sweating.

With all five people—and one pig—finally across, FP sniffed around and made a couple of quick squeaks at Fisher. He was leading the way. Maybe, Fisher thought, he would lead them to an exit. Sure enough, a path opened in the trees in front of them. There was nothing to do but go forward.

The path ended at the base of a massive stone building.

It was made of what looked like cream-colored stone and constructed in a series of steplike levels, much like a Mayan pyramid. The stairs ascended almost all the way up the pyramid, but came to an end at the second-highest level. There was no apparent way to reach the top level.

After what seemed like forever, they finished their climb. They all stopped and looked around, not quite sure what to do next. They could see the sprawling metal jungle below them and the pyramid's unreachable triangular top above them, but no obvious route of escape.

Fisher noticed that the top level of the pyramid was actually a film production booth, surrounded by opaque glass, and encircled with its own narrow balcony, but it was just high enough to be out of reach, even for Dr. Devilish.

"Congratulations," said the Producer over the speaker system. "You've reached the end of the obstacle course. I should warn you, however, that your trials and troubles aren't over; in fact, they've hardly begun. But before I send you all to your doom I think it's at least polite for me to introduce myself."

A door hissed open in the side of the production booth, and a small man emerged, looking down at them from his high perch.

Fisher's breath caught in his throat. His eyes felt like they would freeze solid and fall out of his face.

The man stood with his arms clasped behind his back. He wore an all-black jumpsuit with black, thick-soled boots, and tight, black leather gloves. His thin, dark hair was slicked back from a broad forehead that overlooked a long, hawk-like nose.

Harold Granger. Known otherwise as Dr. X.

CHAPTER 19

Many people say that gardening relaxes them. I have a similar method of relaxation, except that instead of cultivating begonias, I cultivate the terrified expressions of people facing imminent doom.

—Dr. X, Personal Notes

It should have occurred to Fisher that if Two had been able to escape the explosion of the TechX complex, Dr. X might very well have, too.

Specifically, it should have occurred to him *before* he was standing in the middle of a gigantic death maze being stared down by Granger and hundreds of his heavily armed, maniacal creations.

But it hadn't occurred to him. The realization of this miscalculation smacked into Fisher with the force of a manatee on a tire swing.

Dr. X's eyes swept back and forth across his victims.

"Welcome to my new show!" he trumpeted gleefully, opening his arms. He turned to Fisher and narrowed his eyes. "When you destroyed my beautiful TechX compound, I admit I was distraught. Fortunately, I had use of a backup laboratory hidden beneath Los Angeles, full of hundreds of my spectacular creations. And when I heard that *Sci-Fi: Survivor*'s producer had died suddenly, tragically, and inexplicably"—Dr. X coughed—"I conveniently volunteered to step in as his replacement."

"Mr. Gr-Granger?" Amanda stuttered out. Her mouth was hanging open.

"You—you know him?" squeaked Kevin Keels.

"Harry?" Dr. Devilish and GG McGee said simultaneously.

"You know him, too?" Keels said, eyes widening.

"Oh, I know him," Dr. Devilish said grimly. "I've known him my whole life." He gulped. "He's my big brother."

"Your *brother*?" Fisher, Amanda, and Kevin echoed together.

"We weren't what you'd call a *close* family," Dr. X said, letting his arms drop to his sides. "Do you remember, Fisher, when I told you about my early life? How I was tormented and pushed around and beaten up in school? My little brother, Martin, was already bigger than me by then. And you know what he did while those kids were tossing me around like a hacky sack? *He stood there and watched.* Because he was afraid that if somebody hit him in the face, it would ruin his perfectly chiseled good looks." He directed a black stare at Dr. Devilish. "He just stood there and watched, and then scooped me up when it was over and carried me home so that I could help him with his homework. And *she* was there, too," he said, jabbing a black-gloved finger in McGee's direction, "egging them on!"

McGee gasped as though Granger had reached out and socked her in the stomach.

Slowly, Fisher began to understand. Dr. X had brought him here to settle a personal grudge. Why not settle all of his grudges at once? To say that the situation did not look good would probably win the award for biggest understatement ever. And Fisher still had no idea what had happened to Two.

Harold and Martin, aged 12 & 8

"Harry, please," McGee said, clasping her hands together. "I was a kid. I was just teasing you. I didn't mean anything by it."

"Can *anyone* tell me what's going on?" blurted Keels. He looked like he was about to cry. Dr. X turned to look at him, and Kevin shrank backward.

"GG was a friend of mine," said Dr. Devilish. "Neither one of us has seen Harry in years—thankfully. He barely kept in touch after he left for Palo Alto to become a science teacher."

"*Our* science teacher," Fisher put in. "Also a terrifying masked monster with his own research fortress."

Amanda turned to Fisher. Her mouth was still hanging open.

Fisher added, by way of explanation, "That part of his identity wasn't exactly public knowledge."

"If all of you are up to speed," Dr. X said, tapping his foot, "I do have better things to get to, so if you don't mind I'll just skip to the part where I kill you. I am who I am today because of people like you," he said, pointing dramatically at his brother and McGee, "and my greatest attempt at taking over the world was thwarted by you!" he went on, pointing with equal flourish at Fisher. "As for you," he said, turning to Amanda, "I'm sorry that you decided to accompany Mr. Bas here, but now that you've seen and heard all this, I'm afraid I'll have to get rid of you as well. That's what happens when you associate with people like him."

"But, but, what about me?" Keels spluttered. "What have I ever done to you?"

"Nothing specifically," Dr. X said with a shrug. "But I find your music insipid, extremely unintelligent, lacking any kind of artistic merit, and very, very annoying. And I take that *very* personally. So as long as I'm rounding up people for elimination, I figured I'd throw you into the mix." Keels started shivering with feverish intensity. "By the way, the concealed cameras have been rolling ever since the lights came up. *Sci-Fi: Survivor* is going to have the most-watched series premiere of all time, and with the cash I rake in I plan on rebuilding my empire." Dr. X clapped his hands delightedly. "This is the part in which I, the sinister-looking but charismatic show host, explain to you how the final challenge works, so try to look surprised and a little nervous. Perfect! You're all handling that last part splendidly."

Dr. Devilish looked around nervously, probably trying to spot the cameras. He instinctively smoothed his hair behind one ear.

"Oh!" Dr. X said, mocking an expression as if a thought had just come into his head. "I'd almost forgotten something!" He placed two fingers in his mouth and gave a sharp whistle. The door opened and Two stumbled out, pushed along by a very small henchman wearing a black cloak with a hood that concealed his face.

"Two!" Fisher said. His clone looked a little bit roughed up, but mostly unharmed.

"Hey, brother," he said with a weak smile. He looked around at the others. His eyes stopped on Amanda, and his attempt at a smile disappeared. "Amanda! How did you— why are you—" He swallowed. "Why are you *here*?"

"We came to get you out of here," she said, dropping her eyes.

"Basley?" said GG, looking up at Two. "What on earth . . ." She glanced back at Fisher, then back to Two.

"What is this??" said Dr. Devilish, doubling McGee's tennis-ball eyes.

Kevin Keels was too busy trembling and muttering to himself to have noticed the sudden appearance of a second "Basley."

"What's going on?" GG was practically screeching.

"Long story," Fisher said. "If we're not dead later, remind me to tell you."

"Don't worry," Dr. X said, grinning. "You will be." He tilted his head to one side and examined Fisher. It was like being stared down by a bird of prey. "I've been very busy recently, barely sleeping. In some ways I have to thank you. Losing that laboratory forced me to go back to square one, to refocus my creative powers. And, of course,

I got a lucky break." He whistled again, and Dr. X's hench-man, the one who was restraining Two, reached up and lowered his hood.

Fisher actually felt his heart stop. It took a few moments to start beating again, and in the meanwhile Fisher couldn't move, blink, or breathe.

"Say hello, Three," said Dr. X.

CHAPTER 20

I thought I didn't understand what was going on until I had things explained to me. Then I KNEW I didn't understand what was going on.

—Kevin Keels, Diary

"Hello," said the person called Three, in the coldest, least human voice Fisher had ever imagined could come out of his mouth. Out of any mouth.

But it was coming out of his—Fisher's—mouth, or at least a mouth that looked identical. A mouth that sat under Fisher's nose, under his eyes, in his face.

Another clone.

Three's hair was dyed black and slicked back in the same fashion as Dr. X's, and from the way Two grimaced when Three gripped his arm, Three must be a lot stronger than either the original or the original clone.

Fisher wondered if this was a bad time to notice that he actually looked kind of cool with dark hair.

Hair! Fisher's memory leapt back to what at the time had seemed an inconsequential part of Two's escape story: Dr. X had tried to stop him from escaping, and in the process grabbed at him, tearing out a clump of his hair. He'd gotten Two's DNA.

"Two's hair," Dr. X said as though reading Fisher's mind, "was riddled with the AGH hormone. It wasn't easy to harvest it, and I had to work all through the night for nearly a week to replicate our new friend here but, obviously, I did it. Meet the new, improved, and completely evil Fisher. Now I can resume my work. I'll have all the time in the world to bring my greatest dreams to fruition . . . after I eliminate all my distractions, that is." He smiled meanly. Two was looking back over his shoulder at Three, then back at Fisher, his jaw slack, his eyes going wide. Noticing Two's shock, Dr. X began to chuckle. "Why . . . you never even told him, did you?" Dr. X said, wiping away a tear with a black-gloved hand. "Oh, how precious. How absolutely special."

Fisher saw the glow of dawning comprehension fill Two's eyes.

"I had just about figured everything out," Two said, staring at Fisher, his eyes shining with hurt. "But I was missing the last piece . . . I'm not your brother. I'm a clone. Like him."

"You're nothing like him," Fisher said quickly.

Two didn't seem to hear him. "I wanted to believe I was special. I wanted to believe I was . . . I was loved. Stupid."

Two lowered his head until his chin touched his chest. Fisher wanted to say something—anything—to make Two feel better, feel like he was really worth something. But the words just wouldn't come.

Keels twitched. Amanda gritted her teeth. Dr. Devilish had gone the color of chalk dust; GG kept opening and shutting her mouth, like a fish trying to swallow a fly.

Dr. X reached down and pressed a button on his belt. The floor began to rumble, and next to Fisher a panel slid apart in the ground, revealing a long drop down to a dark pool of water. Fisher could make out enormous, even darker shapes swimming underneath its surface.

"These are my new squi-ranhas," Dr. X said. "And before you ask, imagine a creature that can jet rapidly through water and cling to its prey with tentacles like a squid, but with the ferocity and toothy maw of a piranha." Dr. X chuckled. "Or rather, *don't* imagine it. I'll just show you. Three?"

Without a word, Three planted his feet and shoved Two forward. Two's foot grazed the edge of the elevated platform, and he went careening over the side, right past Fisher and Amanda, who leapt to try and catch him. Fisher had to grab her around the waist to keep her from falling in right after him.

"*No!*" Amanda screamed. Fisher watched in horror as

Two plummeted for an unbearably long second before hitting the water.

The pool frothed up. Shapes twisted and swirled for a few brief moments, and there was a horrible hissing and screeching sound. For a second, Two floated up to the surface, on his back, his eyes open and expressionless. The water was red around him.

"No," Amanda kept repeating softly to herself. "No, no, no, no . . ." She slowly sank to the floor, taking Fisher with her, as he released his death grip on her waist.

Fisher felt a leaden coldness spread through his body. The sensation made him want to sink even lower, to lie flat on the floor and then keep on going. He wished he could just close his eyes and sleep for a hundred years, and wake up when everyone who knew him was gone. He had failed Two. His selfishness and lack of foresight had led them to this point. As hard as he'd tried to turn things around, it hadn't been enough.

But a little point of heat blinked to life underneath the cold, just as Fisher was about to collapse and let everything go. Fisher had failed Two, that was certain. But Fisher wasn't the one who killed him. He hadn't created a massive, deadly arena to get his petty vengeance on personal enemies. And the man who *had* done those things was about to take more innocent lives, and go on to do who knows what else.

"That's enough," Fisher said quietly, staring down at Two's body. He felt as though he had gone plummeting into the pool as well. His whole body was numb. He wasn't afraid anymore. He stood up. "That's enough." He stared at Dr. X as dozens of robots began to emerge from the jungle at the base of the pyramid, machines closing in for the kill. *"That's enough!"* he shouted one more time over the din of the approaching robots. He looked straight at Dr. X and yelled, "Kevin!"

"Huh?" Keels replied, still shaking.

"That song, the gift wrap one?"

"What about it?" he asked, his voice squeaky.

"Sing it." Fisher turned to see the massive Tyrannobot begin to lumber up the steps of the stone building. He knew it was only the first of the many mechanical monstrosities that would be on top of them in moments.

"What?" Keels spluttered. "What are you talking about? What's that going to—"

"Sing it," Fisher said. "As loud as you can. *Now!"*

Kevin Keels, pop sensation, moments from being murdered by robots, looked at GG McGee incredulously. She nodded her head.

"Do it," she said.

Keels shrugged, cleared his throat a couple of times, tilted his head back, and opened his mouth wide.

Blueprints for
SONIC BLASTER
based on frequencies
from Kevin Keels's natural voice

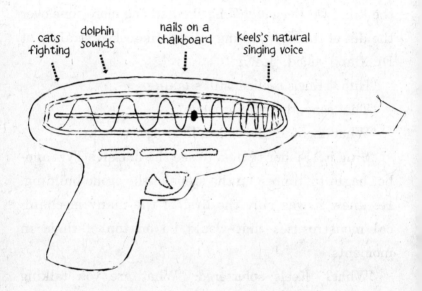

cats fighting

dolphin sounds

nails on a chalkboard

Keels's natural singing voice

"SILVER RIBBON IN A TIDY BOWWWWWWWW..."

If Fisher had known as much about language as he did about physics and biochemistry, he might have been able to select a word that could properly describe what Kevin Keels was doing. *Singing* was definitely not it. He felt like his brain was being struck with a jittery piano hammer.

For a brief moment, he thought of Veronica and felt a pang. She would probably know the proper word. He wished Veronica could hear Kevin now.

He might never see Veronica again.

"UNTIE IT, BABY, BUT UNTIE IT SLOWW . . ."

Fisher threw his hands over his ears. Everyone else did, too. The sonic assault was hitting everyone like a fire hose. Dr. X was on his knees, screaming "Stop! Stop! Make it stop!" Even Three, undoubtedly the toughest of all of them, had his hands clamped on his ears and was doubled over.

"DIDN'T NEED SCOTCH TAPE TO FOLD IT MYSELF . . ."

But the brutal caterwauling wasn't just affecting the humans. Everywhere, the robots were grinding to a halt. As Fisher had hoped, the upper frequencies of Keels's horrible, screeching voice were interfering with their electronics.

"HOPE YOU HAVE A SOFT SPOT SET UP ON THE SHELF . . ."

Alarm bells sounded. Small machines ground themselves into bits and pieces or threw themselves, kamikaze-style, against the pyramid, exploding in a shower of sparks. Fisher knew they only had a moment to act. He looked at Amanda.

"We have to move now," Fisher called over the continued

noise of Kevin's wailing. He pulled out his stretch-tie and eyed the Tyranno-bot. "I'm going to hitch a ride. You do what you do best."

Amanda nodded grimly, hands still covering her ears, and they sprang into action.

≋ CHAPTER 21 ≋

He has a voice that could make people swoon on their feet
. . . . by damaging the inner ear, and deregulating their
sense of balance.

        —*GG McGee, Kevin Keels's Audition Comments*

As Amanda clapped a hand over Kevin's mouth and at last the horrifying wailings stopped, Fisher was already sprinting for the Tyranno-bot. He didn't know how long Kevin Keels's highly destructive voice would paralyze the robots, but he couldn't assume the effects would last more than a few seconds.

After watching Two die, a part of him wanted to curl up on the floor and wait for his own untimely end. He forced himself to shove down the emotions—anger, terror, guilt—that threatened to overwhelm him. He had no time to grieve. He had to stop Dr. X before anyone else suffered or died at his hands.

His mind started firing on all cylinders, looping a single thought back to him: *Fight.*

He wrapped his trusty necktie around his palms to protect them from the heat, and sprang for one massive leg of the Tyranno-bot. Using the climbing skills he'd first honed scaling the Wompalog air ducts, he clambered up the Tyranno-bot's body and straddled its broad iron neck.

Amanda found a section of hydraulic piping that had been exposed when the trap door had opened. Gritting her teeth, she wrenched it out of the ground, then ran to the feet of Fisher's metal dinosaur.

"Can you control that thing?" she shouted.

Fisher looked over at Dr. X, who, doubled over, was being guided back into the booth by Three. In moments, they had reached the door and shut themselves inside. Fisher would have to deal with them later; right now, the army of metal monsters was closing in on them.

"Working on it," Fisher yelled, finding the motor circuitry panel on the back of the robot's head and prying it open. Just as the machine came online again, he yanked out the connection between the main processor and the motor control center. The Tyranno-bot stopped as still as a museum exhibit.

It was a good start. Now Fisher just had to figure out how to make it move again—under his control.

"The machines are at the stairs, Fisher!" Amanda sounded almost excited.

No, Fisher realized. Not excited—angry. Amanda hefted the makeshift weapon in her hands, looking eager to test it out on the first thing that came too close. Fisher risked another glance beneath him. GG and Devilish were still staggering around dizzily, shaking their heads, presumably to clear them of the piercing echoes of Keels's voice. Kevin had collapsed into a ball and had his arms wrapped around his knees.

"Come on, you guys!" Amanda shouted. "Get over here and help me!"

Still moaning, GG and Dr. Devilish staggered over next to Amanda as, once again, the machines began to move.

Dr. X's mechanical servants, electric eyes glowing hot, began mounting the steps of the pyramid. Leading the charge were small spidery robots; behind them were wheeled motorcycle-like robots, and a wide variety of human-shaped robots armed with built-in clubs, spiked chains, swords, chain saws, sharpened propellers, and whips.

And standing against the monstrous army, at the top of the stone staircase, were a TV show host with impeccable hair and teeth, a Hollywood agent who was without sunglasses for the first time in as long as she could remember, a seventh-grade wrestling champion, another seventh grader perched on top of a robotic dinosaur, and a teen pop sensation curled up in the fetal position and crying for his mother.

Fisher squashed a feeling of hopelessness.

"Now, Amanda!" he cried.

Amanda hefted the steel pole like a baseball bat and with one mighty swing sent the head of a spindly droid bouncing back down the stairs to the feet of its companions.

"Nice shot," Fisher said as he got back to work. Beads of sweat popped up all over his face.

"We are all going to die," said Dr. Devilish matter-of-factly as the machines continued their clanking advance.

"We're working on an alternate plan," Amanda said, looking out across the mechanical crowd. "All we have to do is keep them back until Fisher can figure out how to operate that thing."

"What if he doesn't?" said McGee, padding her hands over her suit, probably looking for anything resembling a weapon.

"He will," Amanda said solemnly. If Fisher weren't so busy rewiring a giant metal dinosaur, he would have thanked Amanda for the vote of confidence.

Amanda's head twitched suddenly and she looked around. "Where's FP?"

"Oh, no!" Fisher felt a jolt of panic. But then he saw his backpack, untouched, lying near the Producer's booth, and breathed a sigh of relief. "He's in the backpack. Let's hope he's safe as long as he stays there." He fought back the urge to dismount and grab his pet. But if Fisher abandoned his work now, they were all done for. He put his head down and worked as fast as his tired hands could move.

"Here they come!" Amanda screamed.

The palm-sized insect-bots skittered forward, racing ahead of the remaining force with incredible speed. The first one reached the top of the stairs and leapt straight at Amanda's head. She swatted it out of the sky with her makeshift club, letting out a triumphant yell.

Another one ran up to McGee just as she pulled a large object out of her purse. She crouched down and crushed it with one blow.

"Good work!" Amanda shouted over the now almost-deafening sound of marching machines. And then, swiveling around. "What *is* that?"

"Kevin's latest contract!" McGee replied, hefting the rolled-up sheaf of papers like a billy club.

Fisher glanced down as Amanda crushed two more of the little spider-bots with ease. A third jumped at Dr. Devilish, aiming its eight sharpened legs at his chest. He reached to the back pocket of his suit pants, moving with instinctive quickness, and swept his arm through the air. The thin, shiny object cut the tiny robot in half.

"Titanium comb," Dr. Devilish said, cracking a small

smile. "It takes a lot of work to keep this fine coif in place."

The little robots continued to swarm, and Amanda, GG McGee, and Dr. Devilish swung left and right, shifting from side to side and fighting as hard as they could to keep the insect machines at bay. Amanda missed one and it slashed her across the shoulder, leaving a long, shallow cut. She yelped in anger, then grabbed the robot bare-handed and flung it back down the stairs, where it collided with and demolished two of its comrades.

"Come on, come on, come on," Fisher muttered under his breath. He hastily reconnected a pair of wires, and the ensuing short circuit sent sparks showering in his face. Beneath him, the sounds of battle increased in pitch.

"There's a big one coming!" McGee shouted, pointing at a humanoid-bot. Its long, flexible limbs were tipped with powerful clamping hands.

"This one's mine," Amanda shouted. "Just keep the little ones off me!"

Dr. Devilish and GG McGee backed up to protect Amanda, who dropped her staff as the new opponent reached the top of the stairs. The bot was a foot or so taller than Amanda, with an oval-shaped body propped up on wide-footed legs. Its single, purple-lens eye scanned her up and down, and it extended its snaky, multi-jointed plastic arms to seize her.

DIAGRAM OF
BEETLE-BOT

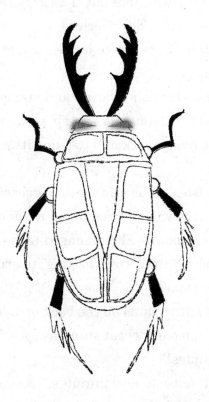

She raised her arms and met its clasping hands with her own, digging in with her heels and pushing. The robot wavered, caught off guard, and shifted its weight to try and force her off her feet.

That was its mistake. There was a reason that Amanda was captain of the wrestling team. As Amanda let herself be pushed down to her knees, the robot leaned farther and farther forward. Timing her motion exactly, Amanda slipped her hands out of its grasp and threw her body into its knees. The machine toppled forward and fell onto its face . . . or where its face would have been, if it had had one.

As GG and Devilish swatted and stomped and flung the little bug-bots, Amanda swung around, putting her knee into the robot's back and twisting its arm behind its metal body.

"I really wish . . ." she said through gritted teeth as she held the thing down and tried to pin its struggling arms, "that you had elbows." She managed to keep it pinioned to the ground with her knee, locking its arms with hers. "Fisher! Now what?"

"Look for a little panel on the back of its neck!" Fisher shouted down, feeling sweat sting his eyes. "I just need a few more minutes!"

"We don't *have* a few minutes," Amanda shouted back. She located the panel, popped it open with an elbow, and quickly freed a hand to yank out every wire she saw. The robot jerked up and down a few times, then lay still.

The main force was on them now. Amanda seized her staff again and began swinging left and right, but there were too many robots, and they were slowly driving her back. Dr. Devilish's comb was snapped in two by a robot that looked like a cross between a dog and a leopard; GG had lost her contract *and* her purse, and all of them were being hemmed in by a wall of mobile steel.

"Fisher!" Amanda cried in terror, as a humanoid robot managed to reach out and snatch away her staff, breaking it in two like a toothpick.

Fisher, watching from above, remembered the bewildering language in the contracts GG had offered him. He remembered, too, the way that he and Two had managed to short-circuit a robot in the TechX labs by confusing it, and an idea occurred to him.

"GG!" he yelled "Paradoxes! Robot brains can't cope with unsolvable puzzles!"

"I work in Hollywood," GG said smugly. "Unsolvable puzzles *are* my business." She cupped her hands around her mouth, forming a makeshift megaphone. "We would like to offer our surrender!" she trumpeted out. "We wish to set this down on paper, and signify our agreement by signing a written contract. But we cannot agree to your terms until you have shown us the written contract bearing our signatures—confirming our agreement."

"You . . . you will only agree and sign . . . once you are shown the proof of your agreement in the form of your signatures. . . ." the robot said, and a faint whine started to emit from within its metal head. "If you have signed, then you have already agreed, but you will not agree until you have signed, and you will only agree and sign if you have signed, but . . ."

The robot's limbs began to spasm in little flutters, and the whine began to grow in volume and pitch. GG stepped back just as it finally lost control, stomping and flailing back and forth, zigzagging across the platform, sending three other robots tumbling down the steps.

Fisher wiped sweat out of his eyes with one hand. *Come on.* He'd never seen a circuit so complicated before. He imagined Two next to him, saying: *You can do this.*

A slender-looking robot with long blades for hands lumbered toward Dr. Devilish. Devilish, weapon- less, backed up until he bumped against the leg of the Tyranno-bot.

"Sayonara, sweet world!" he cried dramatically. "Remember me well. And remember me as extremely attractive." He swept a hand through his hair, placed his hands on his hips, bracing to meet his end, and let loose the gleaming, sunbeam smile that had made him famous.

The robot stopped. The little iris lens opened and closed, blinking what appeared to be long, iron lashes.

"Well, that's interesting," Devilish said. The robot continued watching him.

"You know," he said, keeping the smile firmly in place, "we really don't *have* to fight." He took a cautious step forward. "Just because I'm a human and you're a machine doesn't mean we can't get along. And really, just because you're a robot doesn't mean you don't have a heart. . . . Well, I guess it does mean you don't have a heart, but you have batteries, right?"

On either side of him, Amanda and McGee were whacking robots apart with anything they could find, but Dr. Devilish managed to maintain his composure, his smile, and his charm.

"Look deep into your . . . batteries," he said, sidling directly up to the robot. "You don't always have to do just what you're told, do you? Can't we be friends?" He slowly put his arm around it. "After all, we . . ." His hand found the panel on the robot's back and with two lightning-quick motions, he flipped it open and pulled out a fistful of wires. Immediately, the robot collapsed.

But there was no doubt about it: the machines were winning. And still, they continued to surge up the stairs.

"There are too many of them, Fisher!" Amanda shouted exhaustedly. A robot armed with a spinning blade made straight for her, and she barely managed to dive out of the way as it swung in again. "We can't hold them off anymore!"

Come on, Fisher. You can do this. Fisher inhaled and connected two wires. A spark fired; and then, all of a sudden, he felt the Tyranno-bot begin stirring and rumbling underneath him, coming back to life.

Thump. Thump. Thump.

Every step that the Tyranno-bot took sent shudders through Fisher's spine. "Easy, boy," he whispered. He held a bundle of crossed wires and loose circuitry in one hand. With his other, he gripped his Extendo-tie, which was looped around the beast's head like a horse's bridle. "Easy." Adrenaline raced through his system as two and a half tons of high-carbon steel followed his commands.

"Fisher!" Amanda screamed, ducking the blow of a double-whip android.

"Charge!" Fisher roared. Using his jury-rigged controls to steer, Fisher directed the Tyranno-bot straight for the robot attacking Amanda. The Tyranno-bot delivered a steel-shattering stomp that almost knocked Fisher off his perch. When it withdrew its enormous metal foot, nothing remained of the robot but a pile of scrap and a plume of smoke.

"Thanks," Amanda called up shakily. Fisher gave her the thumbs-up.

Then he pivoted the Tyranno-bot and stomped right into the middle of the robotic force. Fisher felt the impact as a tail swoop knocked a round-bodied axe-bot through the air, colliding with two others and sending all of them tumbling down the stairs with showers of sparks and gouts of flame. His stomach leapt as he made the beast's head plunge down, and there was a powerful jolt as its jaws ripped a many-bladed android in half.

Fisher twitched his hand slightly and the Tyranno-bot's tail swung out and bashed two of the whip-armed androids to pieces. The spider-bots were trying to crawl up its legs to pry Fisher from his perch, but GG, Amanda, and Dr. Devilish kept them at bay. He looked back and saw Three emerging from the Producer's booth with some kind of metal suitcase.

Then, out of the corner of his eye, he saw one of the spider-bots zoom past Amanda and crawl up to the knee of the Tyranno-bot. Before Fisher could scream or react, it leapt straight for his face.

"SquuueeeeeeeEEEEE!" FP flew out of nowhere, clamping his powerful jaws around the spider-bot and crushing it to bits. He made a circle in the air and landed on the Tyranno-bot's head.

"Good to see you, boy!" Fisher shouted. "Thanks for the assist! Now let's finish the job!"

The robot army was crumbling. GG McGee, Dr. Devilish, and Amanda had all picked up fearsome weapons—blades and metal clubs that had broken off the malfunctioning robots. They were cutting down the few stragglers that Fisher and his Tyranno-bot had left in one piece.

"We did it!" Amanda shouted. "We won!"

Fisher cheered. He hugged FP tightly, and his pig squealed with happiness.

Then he felt the force of an impact that almost knocked his eyeballs out. A gigantic *boom* resonated throughout the room. A hole the width of a salad bowl had appeared in his Tyranno-bot's head. The robot started to wobble on its feet, and then sagged to its knees. Fisher, clutching FP, managed to jump off before it collapsed completely onto its side.

"Have you ever seen one of those movies," said the cold, expressionless voice of Three, "where the villain has an elaborate, strange-looking device that the heroes manage to thwart with their cunning and determination?" He was standing on the balcony outside the Producer's booth, and holding a huge, smoking object in his hands.

Three continued, narrowing his eyes: "And didn't you ever think to yourself, 'You know, if the villain just had a *really big gun*, it would make things much easier?'"

He thumbed a button on his really big gun, pointed it straight at Fisher, and smiled. "Well, so did I."

CHAPTER 22

Point me in a direction and pray that nobody you care about is in front of me.

—Three, First Words

Fisher tore his eyes from the enormous barrel of Three's gun and looked around at his companions. Amanda's hair was wild. One of her sleeves was torn almost completely off, and she brandished a sickle-shaped blade in bruised hands. Dr. Devilish had a shallow cut from his upper cheek to his chin, and his suit jacket was missing completely. His hair, on the other hand, was in perfect order. GG McGee's green suit was stained black with machine oil.

Kevin Keels had passed out again, flat on his back.

"I'm sorry, Amanda," Fisher said. He felt his throat squeezing shut. "I'm sorry to all of you. If it hadn't been for my actions, Dr. X wouldn't have escaped. And this thing"—Fisher nodded at Three—"wouldn't exist in the first place."

"Keep it together, Basley," GG muttered. "Don't crack up now." Both of her hands were raised and she was grinning stupidly in Three's direction, as though hoping to charm him out of firing his gun. She obviously had not processed the fact that Fisher was *not* Basley.

"You really don't have to do this," Amanda crooned to Three in the voice she sometimes used on the debate team when an opposing team member was getting overly emotional.

"Occam's razor," Three said crisply, almost cheerfully.

"Occam's *what*?" Dr. Devilish spluttered, then drew back as Three turned the gun on him.

"Given multiple solutions to a problem, the simplest solution is most likely best. There are few things simpler than pulling a trigger." Three smiled, and turned the gun back on Fisher.

"I can think of *one* thing," said a voice from behind Three. Three frowned and turned around.

But not quickly enough to avoid the fist that smashed across his jaw. Three took a single, staggering step and collapsed to the ground out cold, revealing the proud face of Two.

"Two!" Amanda shouted. She dropped her weapon and ran up to him as he jumped down from the balcony of the Producer's booth to meet her. She nearly knocked him over when she reached him, wrapping her arms around him like he was full of helium and would float away if he weren't held down. He gasped out a shallow breath before returning the embrace.

Fisher was completely speechless. He tried to say

ENTERTAINMENT NOW

Special Event!!!

KEVIN KEELS and
DR. DEVILISH
—two beloved stars—will be
signing autographs at dawn today in

STUDIO LOT 44,
the very place that

SCI-FI: SURVIVOR
is being filmed.

something and felt a weak sputter of air leave his throat. As Fisher rose unsteadily to his feet, FP dashed up to Two, and started to gnaw on his ankle. But it was, somehow, a *loving* ankle gnaw.

"What—? How did you—? How in the world—?" Amanda stuttered.

"We saw you get eaten!" GG trumpeted.

"You saw what I wanted you to see," Two said, grinning. "Or rather, what I wanted Dr. X to see. I had a bunch of Spot-Rite sample packets in my pockets—strawberry flavored. Red as blood. I ripped them open and the squiranhas went crazy for it. I guess they weren't too hungry for meat afterward."

"But . . ." Fisher shook his head wonderingly. "You really looked dead!"

"I know," said Two proudly. "Not a bad performance, right?"

"Oscar worthy."

Dr. X's voice sent a chill down Fisher's spine. He had emerged from the Producer's booth, and his eyes were narrowed with hatred. "It's too bad you won't be around to receive your nomination." He picked up Three's weapon and leveled it at Fisher.

"Ah-ah-ahhh," Two said, shaking his finger in the air. "When I was climbing back up here from the pool, I found a backup computer terminal. I took the liberty of posting a special event invitation on the *Entertainment Now* website. Kevin Keels *and* Dr. Devilish—two beloved stars— will be signing autographs at dawn today in Studio Lot 44, the very place that *Sci-Fi: Survivor* is being filmed. The crowd will be gathering as we speak." Two grinned.

"If anything happens to us now, there will be thousands of witnesses."

As if on cue, the distant sounds of screaming, clapping, and squealing began to penetrate the walls of the studio.

"I could kill all of you before they enter the building," Dr. X snarled.

"Maybe," Two said, "but you'd have a big mess on your hands and a lot of explaining to do. When celebrities disappear, everyone shows up to ask questions. The fans, then reporters, then police . . ."

Dr. X hissed through his teeth in frustration. The crowd noises got louder, and they heard exterior doors opening. Voices echoed toward them through the vast space. "Kevin? Kevin, I love you!"

Kevin, who was still passed out on his back, kicked out one leg and muttered sleepily, "I love you, too."

For a second that felt like an eternity, Dr. X kept the gun pointed at Fisher's head.

"Clever," he said at last, lowering Three's gun. Fisher let out a breath he hadn't realized he'd been holding. "On the other hand, nobody will care, or even notice, if *we* disappear. I believe that's our cue."

Without another word, he helped a still-groggy Three to his feet and back to the Producer's booth, using one hand to keep the weapon aimed at Fisher and his group until they'd slipped through the door. They heard what sounded like a metal door clanking shut, and then the Producer's booth began to sink. Like a high-speed elevator, the triangular structure disappeared into the pyramid, where it would no doubt take them down to a secret exit.

Once again, Dr. X had planned for everything.

Fisher clenched his fists at his sides. Granger had come back from defeat before, and he would do it again. And now there was a warped, dark duplicate of Fisher by his side.

For a moment, there was silence, except for the continued sounds of squealing and babbling that filtered in to them from the parking lot. Dr. Devilish was fixing his hair with one shaking hand. GG McGee was rubbing her eyes, as though expecting her vision to clear and reveal a totally different scene. Kevin Keels had woken up thanks to a determined hoof-prodding by FP.

"Basley," said GG, looking at Fisher, "will you please tell me what is going on?"

"I'm not Basley," Fisher said. Immediately, he felt a little better, as though he'd just been given permission to take off a fur coat in July. "He is." He pointed at Two, whom Amanda had finally let go of, although FP was still nuzzling one of his calves. Keels was starting to stir.

"But earlier you said that—"

"Earlier I *lied*!!" Fisher burst out, making GG jump. "I lied, and nearly got us all killed. I'm not lying anymore." He walked up to Two and bowed his head in shame. "The simple fact is that I made you. I wanted somebody else to live my life for me, because I didn't have the strength to live it myself. I can't apologize enough."

"No," Two said, his face turning grim. "I don't suppose you can. I've had a lot of time to think since I escaped TechX, Fisher. Quite a lot. It's embarrassing that I didn't figure out the truth sooner. But what can I say? I wanted to believe."

Fisher was physically shaking. Every muscle in his body ached, and his knees wavered like their caps had disappeared. He had been expending so much energy, gone through such constant stress, to keep his secret. Now that it was finally out, it felt like a hundred ropes pulling him in different directions had all been severed.

"Just a few more things I need to clear up," Two said, crossing his arms. "The woman I've been calling our mother—she's not really our mother."

"No," Fisher said. His face was heating up.

"She was just . . . a person on TV?" Two said blankly.

"Yes," said Fisher, feeling like someone who'd made a career out of knocking ice-cream cones from the hands of happy children.

"And you've been trying to keep my existence secret," Two said.

"Yes," Fisher choked out.

Two stared at him with an expression Fisher couldn't identify. "Is that why you were so desperate to get me back to Palo Alto?"

"Yes. I mean, that's part of it." Fisher swallowed. "The aftermath of the first incident with Granger made the government agency Mom's been working with freak out a little. They're concerned about possible security breaches everywhere. The unauthorized possession or use of the AGH has been made punishable by decades in prison. They noticed the sample, which I used to make you, missing from her batch and dispatched a team specifi-cally tasked with locating the person involved in such a crime."

Two said nothing. He just stared at Fisher, his mouth set in a thin line.

"Hello?" a voice cut through the quiet.

Everyone turned in its direction. There was a man standing near the top of the stairs.

It was Henry. The sound guy from *Strange Science* who moonlighted as a DJ.

"What in the world are you doing here?" said Fisher, jaw sinking.

Henry chuckled. "I was on my way to save you, but I guess you didn't need the help."

≋ CHAPTER 23 ≋

Los Angeles is a city where anything can happen, and it doesn't make a habit of asking if you're ready.

—Two, Personal Journal

"*Save* us?" Fisher said. "But how did you—Why did you—?" He shook his head. "Just who are you, anyway?"

"My name's Syd," said the man formerly known as Henry. "Special Agent Syd Mason." He flipped a slim, black wallet open, revealing an FBI badge. Fisher's heart must have been getting tired of stopping; this time, it decided to try and escape right through his chest. Fisher had just faced down an army of mechanized destruction and gotten through it, only to come face-to-face with imminent doom.

"FBI?" Dr. Devilish said. "Have you . . . have you been pursuing my brother?"

"He was *one* suspect in my investigation," Syd said, taking a step forward. Fisher instinctively took a step backward. "We've been tracking an extremely danger-ous chemical compound, which seems to have come into the possession of one or more civilians." He seemed to be deliberately not looking at Two. "We knew that Dr. X was somewhere in the city, but we didn't know where. Fortunately, I had a special insider working for me—a mole that no one could have suspected."

Fisher was puzzled for a moment, then turned and gaped at the barely conscious Kevin Keels. "*You??* You're working for the FBI?"

Syd turned to look at Keels, then broke into a powerful, roaring laugh.

"No, no," he said, still recovering. "That would have been disastrous. . . . No offense, kid." Keels wasn't quite yet aware enough to understand what was going on and nodded in confusion. "It was . . . Oh, look, here he comes now!"

Syd pointed as a small, revolving panel opened in the floor, and out popped Wally the Wombat.

"Wally?" Fisher said. "Your mole was a *wombat*?"

"That's right," Syd said. "I suspected that Granger would go after the two of you," he said, indicating Fisher and McGee with his head, "and that he might try to lure you to him by taking possession of your own animal friends. I outfitted Wally with a tracking device, hoping he'd get snatched up along with the other two. Speaking of which . . ."

Molly the Maltese hopped out from behind Wally, and ran to GG McGee, yipping excitedly.

"Molly!" GG shrieked. "Oh, my Molly!" She crushed

the little dog in her arms to the point that Fisher feared for the dog's life.

"It looks like he's got something for me, too," Syd said, as Wally ran up to him with a small object in his teeth. Syd took it and held it between his forefinger and his thumb.

It was a test tube. Fisher held his breath as Syd took a small metal box, containing a single syringe, out of one pocket. He inserted the syringe into the tube and studied it carefully.

"AGH," he said, then looked at the measurement on the side. "Exactly one centiliter." Fisher stifled a gasp. Wally must have retrieved Granger's replicated sample.

Syd nodded. "This is what I came for. As far as I'm concerned, the investigation is closed. Some of my fellow agents, as lively as they may be on the dance floor," he winked at Fisher, "are rather more ruthless than I. They're insisting that we pursue the matter further, not only retrieving any samples of the substance, but closely following any reports of its use, and retrieving any *results* of that use for further study." He finally turned his head to regard Two. "But this is my investigation. I'm in charge, and I say it's over."

Fisher felt warmth slowly, cautiously start to flow back into his face.

"That said," the agent went on, "Dr. X is still at

Plans for
AUTOMATIC DANCE SHOES
for the upcoming fall formal

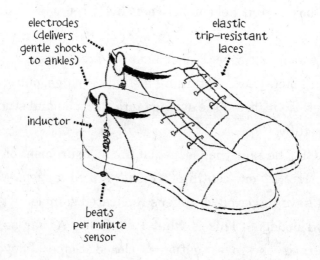

electrodes
(delivers
gentle shocks
to ankles)

elastic
trip-resistant
laces

inductor

beats
per minute
sensor

large, and it's anyone's guess what he might be planning to do next, or where he'll show up. You *twins*," he said, smiling knowingly at Fisher and Two, "seem to be pretty good at taking him on. If you come up against him again and need some backup, just give me a call." He deftly slipped a card into Fisher's hand with his name and number. "Well, I should be going before that big crowd gets here. Take care, all of you. Come on, Wally."

Without another word, he turned and walked back

down the pyramid, his wombat companion close on his heels.

Fisher stared after him. That was it. The last of his problems just walking away. . . .

Well, *almost* the last. Dr. X was still on the loose. And there was still a newly enlightened, very angry clone to try and talk to. Even as the thought entered his head, Two walked up to him. He looked surprisingly calm.

"Listen, Two—" Fisher started to say, but Two cut him off.

"When Granger kidnapped me the first time," Two said, "you didn't have to save me. Dr. X would have killed me, and you would have gone on with your life. You could've just left me there."

"No," Fisher said, "I couldn't have."

"I know," said Two, and to Fisher's amazement, he actually *smiled*. "You may have lied about a lot of things, but Harold Granger really is a deranged, twisted maniac with dreams of world conquest, and we'll have to work together if we want to stop him for good."

Two extended his hand. Fisher looked down at it, speechless. He couldn't believe that the explosion of anger had never come.

"At first I thought of you as just a clone," Fisher said, his voice barely above a whisper. "But now . . . you're the best brother anyone could ever have." He glanced to the side and saw Amanda's eyes watering up. She quickly turned away, scowling. "And she may not exactly know who you are yet, but I think you'll find you do have a mother who loves you. And a father. I mean, they might kill *me*, but I'm sure they'll love you. Can you really forgive me?"

Two's expression hardened. "When you made me, it was completely selfish and ridiculously immature." Fisher winced; what Two said was true, and he knew he deserved it.

"You weren't thinking about anyone or anything but yourself," Two went on. "And yes, I forgive you. Otherwise, I wouldn't be here, would I?" His face split into a wide grin. Fisher took Two's hand, and they shook.

"I promise," Fisher said, "you won't be a secret anymore. I know that you came to LA because you wanted to be your own person. And you *will* be."

Dr. Devilish was staring at the two of them like they'd just sprouted opera-singing jungle vines from their noses. GG McGee just shook her head dazedly. Kevin Keels was running his hands all over his body as if to confirm and reconfirm that all of it was still there and that he wasn't dreaming.

Amanda walked up to Fisher and Two, arms folded.

"You two are going to need some assistance if you want

to take Dr. X down," she said. "I think I've proven on this little adventure that I can hold my own in a tussle. What do you say?"

"I'm sure we'll keep you in the loop," Fisher said. "Won't we, Two?"

"Absolutely," Two said, turning a smile on Amanda.

"Well, then," she went on, "since I'll be working with you and helping you take down an evil mastermind, I'm going to have to get to know you a little better. Fisher, I've known for years. You . . . I'm not so sure about." She raised one eyebrow at Two.

"What do you want to know?" Two asked, anxiety creeping into his voice.

"There's a . . . a certain event coming up on the school calendar," said Amanda. "The fall formal. I *suppose*," she said, rolling her eyes up toward the ceiling, "that I could put up with you for the evening, if . . . if you wanted to go with me. So we could talk, you know, and strategize." For a second, she let her confidence slip, and she bit her lip.

"Well . . ." Two began, clearing his throat and starting to smile before wrestling his own face back under control. "I guess that would be okay. You know, if you think it might be necessary."

Fisher averted his eyes and pretended to be fixated on a piece of twisted metal by his feet, as Two and Amanda continued gazing at each other. FP trotted around them in a circle, looking smug. Fisher had been around FP long enough to know what a pig looked like when it was feeling smug. And he had to admit, it was kind of cute.

"Hey," Two said. "Sounds like the adoring fans are almost here. Devilish, Keels, why don't you two go down and start greeting? I'll be right there."

Dr. Devilish waved his hand in front of Keels's eyes to make sure he was still conscious, and then helped him down the long stairway.

"You think we'll be ready for Dr. X next time?" Fisher said, looking out over the smoldering wreckage that now covered the vast studio space.

"Oh, yes," Two said, looking back at him, and then at Amanda. "But he won't be ready for us."

⚛ EPILOGUE ⚛

The very next day, Fisher stood at his locker in the main hallway of Wompalog Middle School. He and Amanda had gotten back just in time for the wake-up call at the hotel, and Dr. Devilish had worked some makeup magic on Two that made him look just different enough from Fisher that they were able to pretend to be cousins. A little hair coloring, some shading and a bit of putty applied to the nose and ears worked wonders. GG McGee had even helped them forge a note from Fisher's parents asking if "Sean" could hitch a ride on the bus back to Palo Alto.

Fisher had promised that Two would have his own life, and he intended to keep that promise. Two understood that. For now, they would continue to keep a low profile, taking turns going to school and eating family meals, and when the time was right they would reveal the truth to their parents, the school, and the world at large. At the moment, Two was too distracted by thoughts of his imminent date with Amanda to be very concerned about it.

Fisher had a more immediate concern of his own:

Veronica. How was he going to explain his bizarre and erratic behavior to her? How would he explain his whole Basley story, his strange moods, his tendency to disappear at the oddest times? He didn't know what he'd say to her about it. Of course, that was assuming that she was even going to talk to him at some point, which might have been an unrealistic expectation.

"Fisher?"

And there she was. Hair falling down around her shoulders like autumn leaves, bright eyes making everything around her seem duller and grayer. She walked out of nowhere as if summoned by his thoughts.

Which was definitely an improvement over Kevin Keels appearing out of nowhere whenever Fisher had thought about *him*.

"Hi, Veronica," Fisher said, searching for something additional to say. Nothing immediately occurred to him, so he just stood there, gaping like an idiot.

Then, to his surprise, she blurted out: "I wanted to apologize." She dropped her eyes to the floor.

"You . . . what?" said Fisher, the second word barely squeaking out of his throat.

"I'm sorry for the way I acted in LA. You know . . . fawning all over Kevin Keels so much," she said. "I'm sure it must've gotten really annoying. I don't really know what got into me. Today I saw a video on You-Tube. . . . Do you know he's been lip-synching this whole time? He has a terrible voice." She shook her head. "What a fake."

Fisher felt like he was standing at the intersection of a dozen rainbows.

"That's all right," he said, barely able to speak past the grin that was spreading across his face. "It's easy to fall for that kind of thing."

"Well, anyway, I'm glad I've seen through it," Veronica said. "And I thought that since Keels hauled me out of every conversation we tried to have, I could make it up to you."

No, Fisher thought. She couldn't possibly. There was no way in the whole entire universe that the next words out of her mouth could be . . .

"Would you like to go to the fall formal with me?"

Fisher didn't immediately answer. He couldn't. He was too busy worrying about his heart rocketing out the top of his head like a surface-to-air missile.

"Would I like to? Would I . . . that is, I would, which is to say, yes, yes, I would like to go." Fisher hoped that the savage beating he had just given the English language didn't make her change her mind.

"Great!" she said, beaming that smile that could keep

an ice age at bay. "Well, I have to get to class, but I'll see you around." Then, with no warning, or at least no warning that Fisher was socially aware enough to pick up on, she leaned in and kissed him on the cheek before turning and walking away.

Fisher felt time itself drag to a crawl, as great golden unicorns leapt from the walls and shot Technicolor fireworks out of their horns and a symphony orchestra blared into life, its melody echoing dreamily down the corridor. So much for the calculation of K. He had never been happier to have his math be completely wrong.

Fisher turned back to his locker. He had forgotten what he was doing there, so he decided to just stand there and smile until he remembered, and he didn't really care how long that might take. He was going to have to figure out what to do about the fact that now both he *and* Two were going to the formal, but for now, it could wait.

For now, just for a minute, he could be happy.

That evening, after Two had snuck out for a late walk to see Amanda, Fisher unpacked his suitcase and chatted with CURTIS.

"What was I gonna do?" the computer intelligence said. "Let the poor kid starve and beg?"

"You still went behind my back," said Fisher sternly. CURTIS had posed online and over the phone as Two's legal guardian and had been the one in contact with Lulu O'Lunney about Basley's contracts and the apartment she'd arranged for him.

"I was doing it for both of your sakes!" said CURTIS. "Imagine . . . a movie star alter ego that everyone thinks is you! You could reap the glory without even doing the work! Slip into fancy parties, big movie premieres, lots of free buffets . . ."

"All right, all right," Fisher said as he rolled up his jump-socks and put them away. "Just don't pull any tricks like that again, okay?"

"I am always lookin' out for you, kid. Remember that. And hey—want to see somethin' else I got for you?" CURTIS opened a browser window and played a video. It was a newly released commercial, and it opened with a scuffle between Wally, Syd's wombat, and GG's dog, Molly. The two circled and pawed at each other around a tall, gleaming spray bottle of the new edible Spot-Rite, trying to claim the bottle as their own, as if it were a freshly grilled steak. Apparently, the stuff was just that delicious.

"All right, you two," a sweet female voice cut in, and the camera panned up slowly as Jenny Nichols leaned down to retrieve the bottle, spraying it gently over the floor. "The new Spot-Rite," she said, turning her eyes to the camera and smiling brightly. "Nothing else hits the spot."

Fisher laughed and looked down to see FP eagerly watching his friends' star performance, curly tail waggling.

"Fisher?" his mother called from downstairs.

"Hang on, CURTIS," Fisher said, walking to his bedroom door and cracking it open. "Yes, Mom?" he called.

"You just got a big, thick envelope in the mail," his mom answered. "It's marked 'Ace McSnout Script.' Who on earth is GG McGee?"

ACKNOWLEDGMENTS

More clone adventures for all to enjoy! It doesn't seem like so long ago that I began typing out the first chapter of *Popular Clone,* and here's the second installment of the Chronicles already, bigger, crazier, and clonier than ever.

Seeing *Popular Clone* in bookstores and online was remarkable and otherworldly. I think it took a long time to sink in simply for being such a new experience. (I started to type "novel experience" just now and then realized I'd be making a hideously bad accidental pun. I'm only mentioning it at all because I know my mother will appreciate it. And as long as I'm being parenthetical, thank you, Mom. You're a great mom. Even if your sense of humor sometimes makes me want to dunk my head in a bucket of powdered limestone.)

Lauren, Lexa, and Beth continue their excellent work at Paper Lantern and remain brilliant and entertaining collaborators. It's rare for me to find even one person who wants to hear about my crazy ideas for characters — like a toaster who thinks he's an English butler — let alone three of them. Greg at Egmont is the same dashing bespectacled rake as usual. Carry on with that, sir.

I could white out most of this volume and fill it with notes, and still not have the research to properly express what I owe to Lilly, and how much she has done to keep my heart and mind afloat. That's an awful mixed metaphor, but I warned you I didn't know how to express it. Thank you, Lilly.

And of course, thank you to my friends. You're all fantastic. Which is why you're my friends.

There's more cloning to come, and I hope you're as excited to see the final installment as I am to finish writing it. Stay tuned!

Turn the page and grab a sneak peek
at the hilarious and fun-filled

Game of
CLONES

THE CLONE CHRONICLES #3

Available in hardcover and eBook from
Egmont USA in Spring 2014

≋ CHAPTER 1 ≋

Scientists aren't the people who always have good ideas. They're the people whose bad ideas make the biggest explosions.   —Fisher Bas, Personal Notes

"The goat ate my pants."

"Are you sure?"

"I was wearing them when I went to sleep. I woke up with a satisfied goat staring down at me, and no pants. Is that enough evidence for you?"

Thus began episode six of the new reality TV sensation *Family Feudalism*, featuring none other than long-separated brothers Martin and Harold Granger, better known to Fisher as Dr. Devilish and Dr. X.

Dr. X, a short and spindly man with a hawkish nose, tried to shoo the goat out of the room while his brother, Dr. Devilish, continued to lament.

"I'll have to spin a new pair from wool," Dr. Devilish said. He was much larger than his older brother, with a jawline that could cut glass, and perfectly straight hair that was almost as dense as the head it sat on. He adjusted his beige cotton long johns. "I'm sure they won't be nearly as formfitting—"

"Okay!" said *Family Feudalism*'s host, Terry Trebuchet, popping into the room in his green, purple, and gold jester's outfit and jangly five-pointed bell hat. The goat turned and stared up at him with wide, unblinking eyes. "Are you two ready to overcome today's challenge?"

"Scarcely a month ago," said Dr. X, his eyes drifting upward, as though he were appealing to the heavens, "I was ready to overcome all of humanity. To sweep across the globe with my glorious robot army. To bring the continents and oceans into my domain, an empire to last ten thousand years . . ." His eyes grew misty.

Terry Trebuchet stared uneasily at the camera. "I'll take that as a yes," he said, with a nervous giggle.

Dr. Devilish clapped his brother on the back. "Don't listen to him. You know how my poor, poor brother gets." He pulled an expression of deep sadness. It was terribly unconvincing, but then, if he were a good actor, he wouldn't be stuck on a ridiculous medieval-themed reality show with his ex–evil overlord brother.

Fisher, who was watching the show on his computer, pushed back from his desk. "This has to be the worst show I've ever seen," he commented to his clone, Two.

Two was a perfect physical copy of Fisher—a small, skinny twelve-year-old boy with short brown hair. The only obvious difference between them was the number of

2

freckles on their noses: Fisher had three, and Two had come up one short.

But considering Fisher had made Two himself in his own bedroom, that detail and Two's left-handedness were pretty minor deviations.

"I just can't believe it," Two said. "Why doesn't Devilish rat out Dr. X? He should be in jail, not on TV. It's been barely a month since Dr. X tried to kill us all. I can't imagine his brother's forgiven him yet." Two carefully inverted his new Onion Detector, which was about the size of a Q-tip. Two hated onions and had invented a tiny reader so that he could surreptitiously be sure there were no onions in his meals—especially if he was about to see Amanda, and breath was a concern. So far, the detector had successfully measured that there were, in fact, onions on Earth. It needed some fine-tuning to be more precise.

"At this point, I think Devilish's career is all he cares about," said Fisher. "Devilish saw an opportunity when Dr. X got deposed by Three. I bet you anything he blackmailed Dr. X into going on the show with him. Knowing Dr. Devilish, I'm sure he can set his personal feelings aside for popularity's sake." Fisher rolled his eyes. Back in Los Angeles, before their last confrontation with Dr. X and his terrifying creation, Three, Fisher and Two had spent plenty of time observing Dr. Devilish. They knew he would do almost anything for fame—including lie for

3

years about scientific credentials. Fisher went on, "It's weird seeing Dr. X like this. No fancy equipment. No fortress. No robots. Just a scared, little man."

Fisher didn't add that seeing Dr. X au naturel reminded him of the Harold Granger Fisher had once known—the middle school biology teacher who had been one of Fisher's only friends.

Fisher pushed the thought out of his mind. Harold Granger had just been an act, a cover story. And so had Dr. X's friendship.

"Speaking of scared," Two said, his eyes still glued to the screen, "you seem a little jumpy yourself."

November was upon them, and that meant it was the night of their school's fall formal. All day, Fisher had felt as if his limbs were filled with a thousand angry hornets. "I've . . . never actually been to a dance," he admitted.

"You'll be fine," Two said. "And if you aren't, you can always hide out in the locker rooms while I have all the fun."

"Gee, thanks," Fisher said, nudging Two's shoulder. They laughed, briefly awakening FP, whose head was inside an empty popcorn bucket. Fisher's little pet pig stirred momentarily before his snoring resumed.

On the show, Terry led the way out of the hut, pointing to a small cart with solid wooden wheels next to a pair of donkeys.

4

"A crucial part of a medieval peasant's life was taking harvested crops to the market town to sell," Terry said. "To do that, they would use a cart, like this one. Your first challenge is simple. Work together to hitch the donkeys to the cart, then drive it to the wooden post at the other side of this field."

The Grangers looked at the donkeys, at the cart, and at each other.

"You start," they said at the same time.

"No, *you* start," they said at the same time.

"I'm an intellectual titan!" Dr. X said. "I should be organizing the effort and you should provide the brute physical force I require!"

"I'm the TV celebrity!" said Dr. Devilish, planting his hands on his hips. "You should listen to what I say."

"What *you* say??" Dr. X exclaimed. "You were a pre-tend TV scientist who did a hair gel commercial with a talking cartoon porpoise!"

"Don't you bad-mouth Pasquale Porpoise," said Dr. Devilish. "At least he never tried to *kill me with robots*."

"Gentlemen!" said Terry. "Gentlemen! You've got five minutes. I think you should get to work, yes?"

The Grangers shot one more nasty look at each other, then stalked in silence toward the donkeys.

"Come here, you filthy *Equus asinus* . . . ," Dr. X muttered as he reached for a donkey's head. In response, the

5

donkey shot a hoof straight into his chest, sending him somersaulting backward through the mud. Dr. Devilish's donkey scampered to the other side of the cart.

The Grangers spent most of the five-minute clock chasing the donkeys around in circles.

"That's it!" Dr. X crowed at the top of his lungs. "I will not be subject to this humiliation any longer!" With that, he pulled a device from his pocket and pressed a button. The show's microphones picked up a very faint, high-pitched hum.

Immediately, the donkeys stopped running.

And started dancing. And where donkeys are concerned, the place where running ends and "dancing" begins is a fine and fuzzy line. Before the timer had finished counting off five minutes, the Grangers were diving over a low post fence to get away from the donkey flamenco.

"I recognize that device!" said Fisher, over the sounds of shouting from both the brothers and the host. "I saw it being tested in TechX. On whales."

"Yup. I watched those experiments," added in CURTIS, the artificial intelligence residing in Fisher's computer. CURTIS closed down the video window and immediately opened a new one that featured a simple face module of CURTIS's own invention. It featured a series of slightly different smiley faces that shifted as he talked to

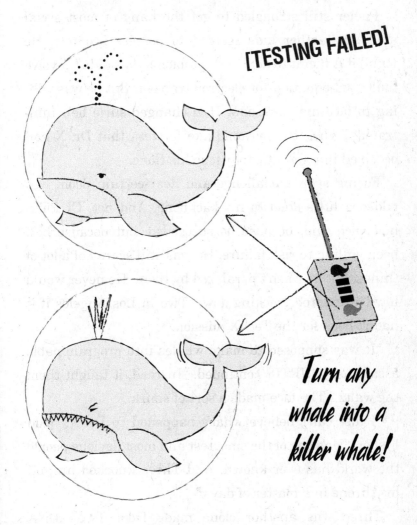

TECH-X
KILLER WHALE DEVICE

[TESTING FAILED]

Turn any
whale into a
killer whale!

Courtesy of CURTIS

7

communicate his feelings. Fisher had taken CURTIS out of TechX with him, and the AI had proven to understand human interaction better than he did.

Fisher still struggled to get the hang of most social skills that other kids seemed to possess innately. He found it difficult to deal with problems that didn't involve multipart equations or electron transfer. But he was willing to face his fears now. He'd changed since he'd infiltrated TechX, the pyramid-like fortress that Dr. X had occupied in Palo Alto, to rescue his clone.

Facing such a challenge and near-certain doom had added a little steel to his backbone. And not, CURTIS had once said, because he succeeded, but because he'd been willing to risk failure. He was still scared of a lot of things, but he wasn't paralyzed by them. He never would have attempted tracking down Two in Los Angeles if it hadn't been for the TechX mission.

"It was supposed to make whales into programmable assassins," CURTIS continued. "Instead, it taught them the waltz." The face made a sort of smirk.

"I just can't believe what's happened to Dr. X," said Fisher. "He's one of the smartest and most devious people the world has ever known. And Three knocked him off his throne in a matter of days."

Three was another clone made from Two's DNA (which was, of course, also Fisher's DNA). He had been manufactured by Dr. X to be a drone: a perfect killing machine. And although Fisher, Two, and Three all resembled one another physically, Three was a horribly distorted version of the two brothers—with no morals, scruples, or feelings, and a single driving desire: power. Dr. X had, for once in his life, miscalculated. He believed he could control Three. He had been proven wrong.

"He must have been planning a takeover from the start," Two said grimly.

"I almost feel sorry for Dr. X," Fisher said. Two shot him a look, and he repeated, *"Almost."*

"Fisher?" came his mother's voice as the door opened with no warning. Two dropped to the floor and rolled under the bed like the room had caught a hail of gunfire.

"Oh, hi, Mom!" he said, spinning in place and trying to look as normal and casual as possible.

"Just brought you up some clean laundry," she said, setting down a laundry basket that ordinarily could walk up the stairs by itself, but had been malfunctioning lately. "Looking forward to the dance?"

"Yep," Fisher said. But the reminder sent a twinge of fear through him. "Should be a great time."

His mother smiled and walked out, closing the door behind her.

Two crawled out from under the bed and leaned against a wall. Instantly, Fisher could tell something was the matter. Two's arms were crossed and he was scowling.

"Two?" said Fisher. "What's up?"

"Nothing," Two said, whipping around to face him. "Nothing at all. Why, you ask? Because the world doesn't know I *exist*! So how could anything be wrong? *No one knows I'm even real.*"

"Two," Fisher said cautiously, "we've talked about this. . . ."

"I'm tired of talking," Two cut in. CURTIS's dot eyes moved back and forth nervously between Two and Fisher. The face window closed to give them the illusion of privacy. "You promised me you'd tell the truth weeks ago."

"I know," Fisher said, sighing. "But I just . . . haven't found the right time yet. Or the right way."

"The right time," Two grunted. "The right way."

"It's true," Fisher said. "This is something we need to plan carefully." CURTIS subtly opened the video window again as a preview for the next episode of *Family Feudalism* came on.

"I'm sorry, Fisher. I can't quite make out what you're saying," Two said, stalking to the other side of the room. "All I'm hearing is *bawwk, bawk, bawk, baaaawwwk. . . .*"

"All right," he said, collapsing onto his bed. "You're right. I'm scared. But that's not the reason we should wait."

"Waiting isn't helping us. Look, you said it yourself," Two said, beginning to pace the small room. "Dr. X is one of the smartest and most evil people on Earth, and Three seized power from him in less than a month. Three's more dangerous than even we imagined. He could be anywhere, planning anything, and he's got all the resources Dr. X used to control. We need to get out there and find him!"

"I know, I know," Fisher said. "And we will. Soon." He looked at the clock. Almost 6 P.M. "For tonight, let's just try and have a good time at the fall formal."

"That's another thing," Two said. "You get to go to the formal in a tux while I have to wear *that*." He pointed to a corner of the room, where a multicolored, feathered monster was propped against the wall. The suit had started its life as the Furious Badger, Wompalog Middle School's old mascot. Two had converted it into a double-billed yellow-bellied bilious duck suit to protest the King of Hollywood restaurant's invasion of the ducks' habitat, and the duck had been adopted as the school's new mascot.

"We made a deal," Fisher said, standing up. "I'm the one that's been going to school for the last three weeks—five, if you count the time you spent running around LA—while you were doing whatever you wanted to do. I go to school; I get to go to the formal as me. At least Amanda knows what's going on. She'll understand. I have to keep lying to Veronica."

"You don't *have* to," Two said. "You could tell her about me. You could tell everyone."

"Please let's not get back into this," Fisher said, rubbing his forehead.

Two looked at the DBYBBD costume and frowned. "Fine. But you're the giant clown duck next time."

"There won't be a next time, Two," Fisher said. "I promise."

"Promises, promises," Two muttered.

Fisher and Two brushed their teeth, combed their hair, and donned identical suits. Then Two sighed and climbed into the duck suit. While Fisher walked downstairs and out the front door, Two placed a remote-activated ladder out Fisher's window and slunk around the back.

By the time FP stirred and woke, Two and Fisher were long gone. The little pig pulled his head out of the bucket and looked around, sniffing the air. Then, realizing there was a leftover unpopped kernel in the bucket, he spent the next hour trying to reach it before again passing out in exactly the same position Fisher and Two had left him.